TIN CAN

a novel by

Allen Leonard Meece

Proudly self-published by KwestHouse.

Uniform Code of Military Justice

ARTICLE. 94. MUTINY OR SEDITION (b) A person who is found guilty of attempted mutiny, mutiny, sedition, or failure to suppress or report a mutiny or sedition shall be punished by death . . .

Nowhere in the UCMJ does it instruct how to quit the service and it considers that walking away from an unconscionable situation is simple desertion and:

ARTICLE 85. DESERTION (a) Any member of the armed forces who—(1) without authority goes or remains absent from his place of duty with intent to remain away therefrom permanently; . . . (3) . . . is guilty of desertion. (c) Any person found guilty of desertion or attempt to desert shall be punished, if the offense is committed in time of war, by death . . .

It's true that a man can go over his commander's head and lodge a complaint with the commander's boss, but if, as is the case with the incidents portrayed in this book, the boss had ordered those incidents, (with the approval of the president!), the complainant would be persecuted to hell.

Thus, the poor enlisted man who hates the crimes which he is ordered to commit is forced to mutiny or to die a little within himself. Remember this, young man, most of the wounds of war come not from the enemy.

DEDICATION

For Rosalind, who dedicated her poetry to me.

For the finest sailors in the world,
Destroyermen and Fishermen.

For those who evaded or questioned authority
or escaped from the Long Binh Jail.

Special thanks to author Sedgwick Tourison
for revealing how spies' covert "military
conflict" became total, evil, war in his epochal
book "Project Alpha, Washington's Secret
Military Operations In North Vietnam,"
St. Martin's Paperbacks, 1997.

CHAPTERS

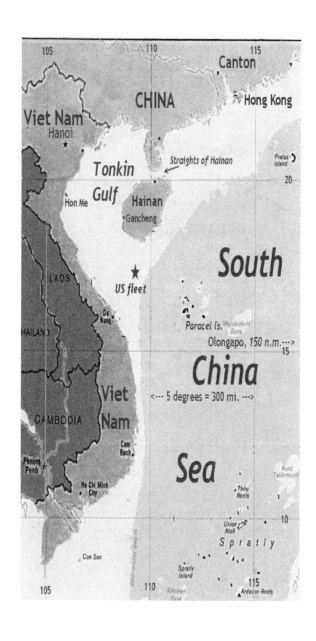

DEPARTURE

THE NAVY WILL TELL YOU IT'S NEVER HAD A MUTINY. But I know differently, I was in one. My name is Mason, John Mason. It was back in 1964 when my destroyer went across the Pacific to start a war. I can still smell the sea. You can call me Jack.

You're standing at the bow of a fast destroyer on the South China Sea at sunset. The ship is long and narrow and sits low in the water and has a tall mast with a big air-search radar turning up high and a smaller, surface-search antenna rotating at the masthead. The bow rises and falls and slices the waves like a meat cleaver. The bow-wave roars up and flares and falls back into the ocean like a big white mustache. Destroyers are called ocean greyhounds and when they're making speed it is called "having a bone in their teeth." It is a pretty sight.

The hull narrows-down to a cutwater no wider than your fist and, standing right above it, you hear the prow delicately hissing and cutting into the ocean. Shuddering when it plows into a swell, the bow surges upward like an elevator and makes you so heavy you can't move your legs. Then the bow passes the crest and quickly drops so that you have to hold on to the lifeline to keep from floating upward. Feels like a roller coaster.

She thunders into a wave and submerges the big white 907's on each side of the bow. That's the number of the USS *Abel*, DD907. DD is the designation for what the Navy calls a general purpose destroyer, a jack-of-all-destruction.

You left the States in the summer of '64 and navigated one-third of the way around the globe to Viet Nam. You'd been as far as Chicago before but this was different, this was *traveling*.

Officers up on the bridge above gun mount 31, the twin three-inch anti-aircraft guns, see you're enjoying yourself and they don't like people having fun. It is better military bearing to be repressed and serious like them. In your boyhood you'd wanted to be like them, "better" than your people who did the hardest work for the least money. Juveniles want to become important and you'd pinned your hopes on getting a free education at the government's expense at the Annapolis Naval Academy. But your eyesight was too weak to pass the entrance examination. Your hopes were dashed. Instead, you went to the Naval Recruit Training Center for enlisted personnel where they taught you that you were inferior to most everyone and very inferior to officers.

One roll of the dice and your lot in life was cast low. You found that you had joined the bottom class of a classist institution.

To appease them, you leave the bow and make your way aft along the four hundred and eighteen foot main deck. You're new on board and want to get to know this powerful machine which is more than a duty station, it's your world until your indentured servitude expires in two more years.

Destroyers are narrow-beamed

and roll more than other ships. You're learning to walk in a bow-legged fashion that keeps your feet under your center of gravity while the deck moves beneath you. It's called "getting your sea-legs" and it keeps you from staggering and getting seasick.

You go by the first of the five-inch gun mounts, mount 51 on the foredeck. The "5" is for the size of the bullet, five inches in diameter. It is a bullet but the Navy calls it a projectile because Alexander The Great called his ballista stones projectiles, or something weird like that. You never know where the Navy gets their names and one story's as good as another. The bullets weigh seventy pounds. You know that because you helped carry them on board and put them in the magazines down near the keel of the ship. The "1" in 51 is for the mount's position on the ship, mount 51 is the first five-inch gun mount from the bow.

Tin Can

It's windy on the forward main deck. You're watching your step and holding the lifeline. The ship's thirty knot self-wind could tumble you down and the officers would see and they'd laugh and one would get to act like a big-shot and chew you out.

Going through the weather-break door, it feels warmer now that you're shielded from the wind. You can smell pork chops frying and fresh paint on the door.

Chuck! Your stomach coughs-up before you can stop it. You dive for the rail as dinner goes overboard.

With your head over the rail, you see the foaming seaway sliding past with the yellow stains you put there. Heh-heh. Happens to everybody, don't get embarrassed.

The wind off the foam is clean and cool. One of the benefits of this job is having the freshest air in the world. You go inside for a drink from the "bubble-up," as the Navy calls the water fountain. The fountain is man-o-war equipment and hums quietly like it'll work even in battle. It's an impressive heavy duty world.

You have a nausea headache but you don't go to your bunk and lie down, you return outside. You want to learn the way of a ship on the sea.

The sun's gone down. It's dark outside. The other two hundred and fifty crewmen are either on watch or are sleeping inside their steel boxes. Feeling alone, like the entire visible sky and ocean belong to you and God, you slowly walk aft in the darkness, making sure of each footstep on the wet steel before taking it. At the middle of the ship, her waist, you pass the boiler room hatch and smell bunker fuel and hear blowers stuffing air into the fireboxes.   Stinging-hot air pours out of the hatch. Your stomach contracts. You step to the rail in case you have to pump bilges again. But you control it and feel okay in a minute and continue aft.

You pass the engine room hatch and hear the furious whine of the big steam turbine engines. You come to understand that your ship is a sea-going power plant with guns on top.

Further aft, you walk below mount 52, which is up on the 01 deck. The "oh-one" deck is shorter and one level higher than the main deck. The contour of 52 stands confidently solid against the stars.

Approaching the stern, you pass beside the third and last of the five-inch gun mounts, mount 53 on the main deck. These are long-range guns called five-inch fifty-fours. The barrels are fifty-four times longer than their diameter, which means they are twenty two and a half feet long. They're accurate out to ten nautical miles, farther than you can see from the main deck. But anything that the range-finder, thirty feet high on the flying bridge, can see, these guns can hit.

She's got more guns aft than forward because her strategy is to speed away from her attackers and open the range to where their guns can't reach her but she can still reach them.

Ahh, it feels pretty good to be a sailor with long guns. With a little bow-legged swagger, you arrive at the fantail, the after end of the ship. It's lurching and rumbling and rattling with the effort of transferring seventy thousand horsepower from the two propellers to the ocean. A maelstrom of white water follows the transom and makes a foamy trail which traces her course for a few miles.

She's a mover, it's her stock-in-trade. Men are sleeping below your feet and the madly whirling props are cavitating five feet below them. The props are carving air-pockets and snapping and banging so hard in the black water that you can feel them through your shoes and your hips and even in your teeth which are buzzing. Hold on to a deck ventilator to keep stability. Stay away from the edge. A sudden lurch could flip you over the lifeline and leave you in the drink while the ship hustles away in the night. There's supposed to be a lifeguard watch back here but you don't see him and there's nobody to transmit a "Man Overboard" and they wouldn't miss you until breakfast.

Looking forward, there's stinky smoke coming from the two stacks and the black mast is swinging arcs through the stars. Wait a minute, something's wrong. The navigation lights aren't on! That's a breach of international collision regulations, better let the bridge know that they forgot something.

Then you remember; she's heading for military conflict. The lights aren't on because she probably wants to sneak up on somebody. Shouldn't be too dangerous. The captain says it's just a conflict. The American free press, the prime democratic requisite for an informed electorate, parrots the same thing. Conflict. Fencing matches? Jousting with cushioned lances? Suction-cup arrows and rubber bullets? Maybe it's like movie battles with explosions that don't kill anybody and always miss the good guys and we're the good guys. Movies have proved that. Americans are good guys. Of that, there can be no doubt.

What the hell is a military conflict? You've never heard the term and you've read a lot. You hope they remember you weigh a hundred and thirty pounds and don't sign you up for a contest that takes lots of beef, like tug-of-war. Will there be chess tournaments? That's a strategy game, it seems appropriate for a military conflict. You could win some points for your side and get a promotion if they have chess tournaments.

Tin Can

The officers have been to college, they'd tell you if there were any and all sorts of killing going on in this conflict. They're smarter, older, better-paid and more respected, they wouldn't lie . . . unless that's why they get that extra income. You've only been to high school and was maybe picking up a pencil you'd "accidentally" dropped on the floor and peeking up skirts when the latest definition of war was given out. You should've paid more attention to lessons than to legs.

Boy, that French teacher though. She stood against the side of her desk and raised one thigh to rest on the edge and sometimes you could see the top of a stocking but never her panties. That was the big prize, to see panties and imagine what was under them. You had a dream about her in the vacant school building after class. She smiled teasingly and went up a flight of stairs. You moved beside the stairs and could see her garter belt and ass and the horny woman wasn't wearing panties and you glimpsed a naughty puff of hair between her legs, umm. You started up the stairs and she was probably headed for the empty teachers' lounge with its big roomy couches and . . . how did it turn out? She probably obeyed authority and didn't let you have what she had. Authority seems to do that a lot. You have a warm crotch out here on the open sea on the back deck of a rumbling warship. When are we going to get some liberty?

In twelve years of schooling, not one teacher had ever suggested that the country is governed by something other than logic and truth. If nobody calls it a war then then it isn't a war, dammit.

But you'd like to understand this "conflict" better, it could prove to have a bearing on your health. With all this lethal equipment around, there are bound to be a few unfortunate accidents that result in... dead servicemen. The government has to bury them and pay insurance and keep records. They can't keep a death a secret. Parents have to be told when their children are gone forever. Maybe it's not a war until a certain round number of participants, say, one hundred, have been killed. When a hundred people have died, then our faithful representatives, the United States Congress, stands up and says "A State Of War now exists between the United States and a Viet Namese political party." Then the fair US Navy probably lets you drop out if you don't think twenty-five dollars a week is worth getting killed for. You made that much on your paper-route, for Chrissake. They probably offer five hundred, or even a thousand dollars a week to stay in the service and maybe die. That would be fair. The Navy says it's fair and you sort of believe it. You're inexperienced.

Now you're wishing it were a real war. You could make some money, buy a good car in a few months. People risking death deserve better cars than civilians playing it safe back in The States.

A wave splashes against the quarter. Spray blows across your face. The wind is coming up. This destroyer is alive, steaming through the night, self-contained, self-controlled and independent. When it's away from home base it's a world unto itself. It sees, hears and feels things in the sky and ocean that a person can't. It has radar and sonar to see far-away planes, ships, shorelines and submarines. It has evaporators to make fresh water from sea water and freezers to feed you anywhere in the world. It has bunks, bathrooms, showers and spare parts for everything that can break or get shot away. It's also an arsenal of explosives; hundreds of five-inch and three-inch shells, six torpedoes, two hundred anti-submarine mortars and a stern rack with eight depth charges. There's a fifty caliber machine gun on board with thousands of rounds stored somewhere and there are rifles for landing or boarding parties and forty-five caliber pistols in the small arms locker.

You're proud of it and glad that it needs you to do some of its thinking. You're a sonarman and know how to find and destroy submarines but oddly, they only pay you a child's allowance. That must be because you're expected to sacrifice money to serve your country. And do mind-numbing maintenance work like scraping and repainting a rusty bulkhead year after year. Funny that there's so little appreciation for all you are giving of your time and freedom and sweat and lost income.

For some reason, they treat you like a naughty boy scout and force your abject subservience. Discipline. That's what they call it. You accept it because your school system conditioned you to obey and believe in authority. Fearing their wrath, you question nothing but you feel a withering of your spirit. More of that noble sacrifice. You obey serious nonsense so you can win the prize of escaping after four years of indentured servitude with some dignity intact.

But sometimes, like now, riding a fast and dangerous ship under all the stars of the Pacific Ocean, you love the damn Navy.

Tin Can

GUNNERY

THE *ABEL* ARRIVES as ordered at the destination of her global navigation; a fishing village on the coast of "Vietnam, Republic of."

She halts and anchors five miles

offshore under the tropical sun. The village reposes in the shade of a few dozen coconut trees. Behind them, filling the entire western horizon, is the hilly blue-green tropical rain forest, the zone of military conflict. The Viet Cong guerrillas have no airplanes to bomb the *Abel* and no artillery that can reach her but the crew begins receiving hazardous duty pay anyway. Ten extra dollars a week.

Ship's routine goes on as usual except for one thing. A powder hoist inside mount 51 clacks and whirs and hoists a projectile from a magazine near the keel and delivers it to the loading tray. A tough old gunner in blue denim bell-bottom trousers, sun-bleached blue shirt and snow-white sailors' hat, steps out of the mount and walks to the end of the long barrel. He unscrews the protective tompion from the bore. Gunners' Mate First Class Goodwin puts his fingers into the gun muzzle like he's testing a shark's mouth. The rifling is smooth and hard-edged. He peers into the bore. The tube is diamond-bright all the way back to the breech.

Satisfied, he goes back inside the mount and turns a red switch from "Off" to "Load." A solenoid snaps, machinery whines, the loading ram drops down, clamps a projectile, swings it up level with the breech and slams it into the chamber. Then it loads a three-foot-long brass cylinder of gunpowder into the breech behind the projectile. The gear-driven breech block swings closed and locks. A red light on the control panel comes on with a baleful glow that reads "Ready To Fire."

The ship has gone from peaceful to hostile with the simple act of loading a gun with intent to fire. The destroyer is set to destroy life and property consisting of huts, canoes and a few childrens' tricycles. And any children that get in the way.

Jack Mason and Gerald Oberhoffen were up on the flying bridge, at the top of the ship's superstructure, looking at Viet Nam through the big pedestal-mounted search binoculars. Jack was a twenty-year-old sonar technician and Obie was a twenty-one year old torpedoman's mate.

"Oh man, Obie, check out the thatched huts and palm trees. Looks like Tahiti."

"Give me a look. Yeah. They've even got outrigger canoes pulled above the high tide line. They're fishermen. I thought I smelled fish cooking."

"I wish they'd let us off to go meet some of the people we're defending. Get some home-cooking for a change and lay out under the palms."

"And maybe get bombed by those warplanes," said Obie, pointing to a pair of American planes that were looping and diving above the hills behind the village.

"Look," said Jack. "There's smoke in the jungle. Must be using napalm, good old jellied gasoline." And then, seriously, "What the hell's war doing in a nice place like this?"

"Hope none of the villagers are up in the vegetable patch while this shit's going on. We might kill'em while we're defending 'em."

"Democracy can be lethal," replied Jack.

"Shh, they might hear us," said Obie, peeking over the rail down to the open wing of the bridge where officers were standing under their visored disk-hats.

"Well, we're stuck now," said Jack quietly. "The only way out is to take the motor whaleboat and go live in the jungle. But it's full of Army guys. Let's go eat."

Obie's face turned grim. "The point of no return. I don't remember voting on this. Did the crew vote to kill while I was away on liberty? Now my choice is to kill or to go to jail. That's democracy?"

"Calm down, Obie, it's like our executive officer says, 'We're not practicing democracy, we're protecting it.' We learned that in boot camp when they even took away our right to a good night's sleep. Remember them banging a cola bottle around in a steel shit can at three a.m. for reveille?

"Yeah, that was the time to get out. Why do I wait beyond the point of no return? Should've wet the bed the first night like those guys who were out of the Navy before breakfast. They probably just poured water on their fart sacks, who would've analyzed it for piss?"

"Well, don't try it now, they'd just make you swab it up and sleep on the deck," answered Jack with a grin.

"Tomorrow morning I'm going to submit my letter of resignation," said Obie, quoting the SEMJ, the

Tin Can

Standard Enlisted Mens' Joke. It was funny because its initials sounded like those for the Universal Code of Military Justice, the UCMJ, which was a real joke. Calling the rules that enforced obsequious behavior a "system of justice" was so sarcastic that everyone laughed at the arrogance.

After the word was passed to knock-off ship's work and after the crew had washed and eaten, sunset fell. The *Abel* went to a darken ship routine that offered no external lights to reveal her location. All exterior doors and porthole covers were closed. The watch on the bridge operated with faintly glowing red instruments. Internal passageways were illuminated by dim red footlights. It was time for resting.

The modern Navy aboard the USS *Abel* segregated into the classist and racist patterns of its original model, the English Navy of Queen Elizabeth I. The crew's mess deck was bright with fluorescent lighting. Off-duty sailors patronized the twenty-four-hour coffee pot and shared gossip, called "scuttlebutt," after the old sailing ships' wooden water casks for the crew to use.

A cook was banging pans in the galley, getting a head-start on tomorrow morning's "SOS, Shit on a Shingle," chipped beef on toast. It was fun to call it that, it didn't mean it wasn't delicious.

The movie tonight had been a good one, "West Side Story." It had made the young men homesick for the places where they had all-too-recently suffered their adolescent rites of passage. The room had been packed with hot bodies but now it was cooling.

The CPO's, chief petty officers, highest-ranked enlisted men, had a small mess deck in the waist of the ship, called the chiefs' lounge, near their sleeping quarters. They could eat, chat and roll off to bed without walking more than twenty feet. They avoided the crew. They were older, secretive and less happy-go-lucky than the workers. They were spending twenty-five years in the Navy for a pension and calling it a career. The men called them lifers.

The officers' mess deck was called a wardroom because they were wardens, as in game wardens or prison wardens. Their mess deck had wooden trim, tablecloths and china plates instead of steel mess trays like the men used. They had stewards of a different race, Philipinos, to cook, serve, clean, make beds and do their laundry. After the stewards attended to the officers' personal needs all day, one steward would pull night duty in a tiny galley called a pantry, until midnight, brewing coffee and cleaning ashtrays and making snacks should any of the sirs get hungry. They lived in a compartment called "Stewards" in the part of the ship called "Officers' Country." The only American crew members who brooked that segregated section were radiomen delivering priority radio messages.

Sonarman Jack came into the crew's mess deck, stood at the bulletin board and read the daily epistle from the Executive Officer:

ORDERS OF THE DAY
1. All personnel are prohibited from possessing or reading the anti-military, un-American novel called "Catch 22" by Joseph Heller.
2. All personnel are prohibited from placing life jackets on the deck as this gets them dirty and makes them less visible in man overboard situations.
Penalty: ten hours extra

duty.
3. Due to paper cups being
left all over the ship, the
coke machine is no longer
free but charges a nickel.
<u>Uniform Of The Day</u>:
Dungarees and white hat. T-
shirts may be worn due to
the warm climate but shall
be kept tucked inside the
trousers. The master at arms
will be enforcing this rule
with extra duty in the
boiler rooms.

LCmdr. Alfred Pinsetter XO,
USS Abel, DD 907

Jack smiled when he saw Val
Scarputti, a quiet and thoughtful boiler
tender, playing two games of chess at
once and winning them both. He went
over to the table and heard Val
explaining stalemate to an opponent.
"Stalemate is like this so-called

military conflict. Neither side can beat the other side but nobody quits. It's a waste of time, lives, money and resources and should just be called off. It's a tie, a draw, a stalemate."

"How'd it get this way?" asked Jack, enjoying Val's candor.

"It already was this way when we sat in for the French. They gave us an old end-game after they'd been checked at Dien Bien Phu. We started in stalemate and we're still in stalemate. Neither side can lose and neither side can win but they still sit there making noise and killing people after the game is over and it's time to just walk away. Big mobile queens chasing devious little pawns through the jungle on a distorted and warped chess board called Viet Nam. We can't capture the pawns because they have sanctuary in tunnels in the jungle, they get to sneak around, hide in trees, dig caves, cross international borders and run away when they get tired. We get to sit on the ocean and on the hilltops and shoot at the trees. It's voodoo, no way to win. Unless you want to get into the genocide game," he said with a grim scowl.

Visibly angry, Val got up and walked away.

Looking scared, the men silently folded the chess boards and put the pieces away. Val was talking seditiously by contradicting and modifying government propaganda. By merely listening to him, the men were commiting conspiracy, organized treason. The military's job is to enforce political ideas so it doesn't allow its employees to comment on the prevailing political dogma.

The seed of knowledge had been placed in the minds of the men around that table. A little of the warrior's edge, which is a craving for victory, was dulled. They would defend themselves if placed in danger by their commander but self-defense can only win the battle, not the war.

"Hey Jack," said Kaiser, a blond-headed gunfire controller who wore glasses and looked more like a high school kid than most of the crew and was playing cards with Obie. "What does the word say? Did the XO say anything about where we are??"

"I don't know, the orders of the day couldn't be bothered with little things like where we are and what we're doing."

Kaiser smiled. "Yeah, all Pinhead does is make sure we know about the price of soda pop, like we can't see it posted right there on the machine."

Obie said, "Well, one thing that's nice to know is that you can always wait for the Stars & Stripes to come out a month later and maybe let you know what you've been doing."

"NOW SET MODIFIED GENERAL QUARTERS FOR GUNNERY!" blared the 1MC, the

Tin Can

Navy's designation for the public address system.

"What's going on?" Obie asked Kaiser, who was getting up to leave.

"It's show-time for shore bombardment," said Kaiser over his shoulder.

"NOW HEAR THIS, ALL WEATHER DECKS ARE SECURED TO UNAUTHORIZED PERSONNEL."

"Let's go to the weather deck and watch," grinned Obie.

"Not me," said Jack with a wink and a yawn, "I'm going to hit the sack."

One after the other, they pretended to head for their berthing compartments but sneaked to the port forward main door and stepped outside behind the weather break. It was a soft tropical night. The forest, five nautical miles to the west, was a dark lumpy silhouette, re-possessed in the night by its natural owners, the Viet Namese. A star shell ignited high in the sky, illuminating the forest behind the village. White-burning phosphorous glared in the sky and made jagged shadows under the coconut palms on the beach.

"Ain't that the ugliest thing you ever seen?" said Obie. "Just like a bad dream. I bet the villagers are pissed-off, being defended from communism this late at night."

"See that little spark way down south?"

"Where?"

"There," said Jack, pointing. "I think it was a muzzle-blast from another destroyer. I think we're on a firing line."

WHAM! The air beside them ripped apart. Their ears rang. Particles stung their faces. The long barrel of mount 51, unseen in the dark, had angled back toward their vantage point and fired. A spent powder case clanged to the deck.

"Jee-sus!" Obie said.

"Key-riced!" Jack said.

Tin Can

They couldn't see where the projectile landed. There was neither explosion nor return fire. At least, the village didn't blow up. Jack harbored a small hope that the ship wasn't trying to hit anybody, was just trying to scare them into submission, a fantasy encouraged by Washington, D.C.

"Does this feel wrong?" Jack asked. "Isn't this, let me see here, what's the right word? What's it called when you shoot somebody who can't shoot back?"

"Yeah," Obie answered. "The word is murder. The Lone Ranger wouldn't do this." He was silent a moment, then added with sad finality, "We're on the wrong damn side, Jack. Shooting little guys in flip-flops who can't shoot back. They're not the bad guys, we are. The Navy lied. You get used to the constant little lies and when the big shining one comes along, you have a tough time knowing if it's bad or not. Well, this looks real bad to me."

You don't want to face the truth. It would capsize your twenty years of conditioning and cast you overboard, alone in the sea of your culture. You grab at the last straw of a drowning man; humor.

"If they told the truth, Obie, nobody but jerks would come over. Just think of this as military job security. They're trying to support their bad habits and ugly families."

Another star shell ignites. They see in stark black and white that neither is smiling.

"So they put Madison Avenue public relations crap all over it, like soda pop and cigarettes," Obie replied.

WHANG! The sucking blast from mount 52 flapped their clothes and blew their hair around.

"Well, this is my life and I'm not going to believe one more stinking word that comes out of their mouths," he said with certitude.

Tin Can

BANG! Mount 53 went off. The ship jolted like a fifty-ton sledge hammer had just been dropped on the stern.

Jack shouted, "You can't believe'em but you gotta act like you do! Let's get some sleep!"

"Get some sleep?" Obie had to laugh. "Get some sleep? Now *that's* funny." He had said what needed to be said and was ready to go forward. He held up Jack's arm like a ring announcer with a winning boxer;

"For the best Joke Of The Day, called 'Let's Get Some Sleep,' the winner is . . . Mighty JACK MAY-sonnn!"

The door beside them began to open. They moved quickly up the ladder to the oh-one deck and hid behind the triple torpedo tubes and peeked over to see who was coming out.

It was the master at arms who was also Obie's boss and chief torpedoman, checking for unauthorized personnel on the weather decks. He stood at the rail and took the scene in. He farted long and low, sure he was alone. He unzipped his pants, took out his pecker and directed a stream overboard. Obie got a big steel battle helmet, held it out over the main deck and dropped it. It landed six inches behind the shipboard cop with a sudden BANG!

The chief torpedoman leaped overboard as quickly as his self-preservation instinct could react.

When he realized the ship hadn't blown up under him, he shouted from the water, "Man overboard! Man overboard! The master at arms is overboard!"

Jack and Obie threw a life jacket in his direction and slipped away to their bunks. The guns were silent for half an hour while the bosuns and gunners left their gunnery stations to retrieve the overboard cop.

Tin Can

Lying on the canvas drum head called a bunk, as the guns resumed firing, Jack took Sonya's letter from under the pillow and re-read the ending; "I hope our baby will have your sense of humor and intelligence. Can't wait to be your wife, Sonya."

BAM! Mount 53. Pity the poor peasant on the other end of that. Pity Sonya for wanting me. Pity me for wanting my buddy's girlfriend, and for getting Sonya pregnant. If it *was* me who got her pregnant. How do I know what she does when I'm at sea? Life's a bitch and then you go to war and maybe die. If life isn't any better than this, then dying may not be that terrible.

The snoring of the other men goes on through the whanging and banging in the hull. Stop trying to understand. Be like them. You can't figure-out this mess.

KA-WHANG! Mount 51, the

loudest, closest to the bunk room. Berthing space, the Navy calls it. Maybe life is all about definitions. Maybe life goes to the winner in the war of definitions. When do I get to define something? I'll define one thing now. This is not a conflict, it is a fucking war and I'm on the wrong side. No, I take that last part back. I'm an American, I can't be on the wrong side.

BANG! 53, back at the stern.

Make up your mind. Something big could've gone wrong again in America, same's it did when it killed most of the Indians and took their land because they didn't have paper deeds and titles and a monstrous standing Army to back them up. Millions of Americans thought that was right. Probably really good people who were one hundred and ten percent sure that they were doing the right thing when they killed people who were defending their land with sticks and arrows against our rifles and cannons.

Tin Can

Congress probably even gave them medals for slaughtering the "savages." *Thinking* you're on the right side doesn't mean anything. You've got to look at the big picture. Take a "world-view," whatever that is. What do you know about world-views? Nothing.

BLAM! That was Mount 52. The heavy recoil is straining the aluminum deck plates on the oh-one deck. You've seen where it was starting to buckle just from a few practice shots.

Now you know this isn't a "conflict" and the Navy's a liar. It takes orders from the government so the government is a bigger, fatter, liar than the Navy. They made it bright and clear that they'd throw you in the brig if you didn't act like you believed everything. A real, true American government wouldn't force its citizens to lie and murder. No no, wait a minute. That means the government's gone crazy. The country couldn't exist if that were true. I am on the right side but the right side just happens to be doing a few wrong things right now, that's all. It'll blow over. It's trying to conduct a civil war in Viet Nam, a backward, semi-civilized country the size of Georgia. Georgia was easier to handle. Georgia was in our Civil War. Thankfully, no foreign superpower intervened in that one. They're telling us that Viet Nam is really two different countries, even though the United Nations didn't split it in two, they only put a demilitarized corridor across the middle of one country. They say we're helping the good half of the country to win. Such bullshit. The lies've passed critical mass. It's time to cover your own soul. You owe them nothing. They'd deceive you right into death and live happily ever after if you let'em. When things get crazy it's every man for himself. These guys snoring through gunfire are how wrong people behave. It's not their fault they're not smart enough to take a world-view.

Tin Can

Their teachers were hired and fired by the same right-wing school boards as yours were. You've figured it out a little bit. You know nothing of the world economy so you can't know that all this insanity is about oil reserves and rubber plantations and raw materials for industry and power trips for big shots. Close your eyes. The true reasons will come when they come.

TONKIN GULF

THE *ABEL* BOMBARDED THE RAIN FOREST for six days and no one talked about the gunnery. The crew ate and slept and worked to the jolt of big bore rifles firing every ten minutes. There was nothing you could say about it. It was Navy policy to shoot people in the woods.

At noon on the seventh day the guns stopped. Jack and Obie went to the fantail to survey the damage. None. The puffy green jungle parasol had swallowed the *Abel*'s shots like popcorn farts.

"Seven hundred thousand dollars in ammunition and what do you get? Broken branches," Obie said and smiled. "You know, they say the U.S. spends ten thousand dollars a head for dead Viet Cong. I bet we just tripled that!"

They laughed at the lethal silliness of the campaign.

"We ought'a give'em each ten grand to stop fighting. Hell, *I'd* quit for ten grand," said Jack.

"I'd quit for ten dollars, if they'd let me. We'll have to work five years to make ten grand. VC's probably don't make that much in a lifetime. Why kill'em when you can buy'em?"

There was no wind. The sea was a slowly-flexing mirror of the sky. A sampan came out from the shore with a US Marine gunfire spotter and six ARVNs, soldiers of the Army of the Republic of Viet Nam. The American went upstairs to talk with the captain while the young soldiers in lumpy combat boots stayed in the boat.

From two different worlds, the big haze gray destroyer and the hand-made wooden sampan floated together on a sea that looked like sky.

Jack tried to be friendly to his comrades-in-arms from the country he was defending.

"You guys Arvin?"

"Yes," one answered.

"You want a cold coke?"

"Yes."

Some of the others smiled. But some didn't, knowing that when they smiled they looked even more like children. Their national draft must be running out of grown boys.

"Obie, let's get these men a drink. They probably haven't had a soda-pop in weeks."

"I'll buy if you fly," Obie said, handing Jack some nickels.

The sodas came out of the machine warm and syrupy. The paper cups were soggy and soft.

"Maybe they'll look better to jungle fighters," Jack thought. He put them on a mess tray and took them back to the boat. He handed the cokes to the soldiers in the sampan. Their sergeant took a sip and spat it out. It ran down the hull of the U.S. warship. Others took a few polite sips and put the cups on the seats.

"They show surprisingly good taste, don't you think, Obie?"

"I guess they're not as hard-up as we thought," answered Obie and walked away.

The Marine came down from

the captain's cabin and got into his boat and went back to the jungle. The big hydraulic anchor winch up in the bow clanked and groaned and weighed the anchor. The *Abel* was free of the bottom.

"All ahead slow," said the conning officer on the bridge.

"All ahead slow, aye sir," answered the lee helmsman. He moved the brass levers on the engine order telegraph which repeated the order in the engine rooms with clanging bells that could be heard above the noise of machinery.

Enginemen moved telegraph levers to "Ahead slow," which rang answering bells on the bridge. Then they manually opened the throttles, big red wheels on special valves which opened the steam pipes to the turbines. A muffled screech came from deep in the engines as steam blasted against whirling turbine blades. Roller bearings began rumbling as the two heavy prop shafts started to turn.

"Right standard rudder," said the conning officer.

"Right standard rudder, aye sir," answered the helmsman, spinning the wooden steering wheel clockwise. The rudder indicator showed the hydraulic rams down in the fantail were swinging the twin rudders to the right. The *Abel* swung around to a northerly course and began the graceful motion of moving over the sea swells. To the north lay the Tonkin Gulf, a big but shallow bay claimed by northern Viet Nam and China.

The crew didn't know where they'd been or where they were going. The captain knew they were going on a covert operation, a "DeSoto Patrol," but he didn't tell anyone but the department heads and he told them to keep it secret from the men he was taking there.

First the ship needed some fuel. For all its self-sufficiency, the ship's endurance is limited by its appetite for fuel. Forty-eight burner nozzles, spraying many gallons per minute of bunker fuel into the fireboxes of four boilers can empty the fuel tanks in a week. Being in a war zone and ready for action, the *Abel* must keep her fuel tanks topped. She refuels every other day, usually at night when the men would rather be resting.

At 2200 hours the off-duty section is in their bunks and the night watch has been set. In good weather, the night watches are dim and quiet, comfortable and clean, something like a poor man's sea cruise.

"NOW SET THE SPECIAL SEA DETAIL FOR REFUELING AT SEA!"

Those who have sea detail assignments get up cursing and go on deck and don life jackets and stand by to receive fuel from another, bigger, ship. The Fox Division "smart boys" handle the high line, a hawser with a trolley to transfer supplies and personnel between ships. They go to the oh-one deck and lay against the bulkhead and try to reclaim a few minutes of stolen sleep. They work at ship's maintenance all day and stand four hours of watch at night and refuel the ship every other night.

The destroyer maneuvers behind the tanker, matching its speed and course and slowly draws alongside.

Obie says in his Missouri drawl, "You know, the doctors say that a man loses a week of his life-span every time he doesn't get a good night's sleep."

"Is my hair turning white yet?" Jack replies.

The red work-light on the mast shows Obie's grin. "They're gonna think I'm weird back in Sedalia when I get up at midnight, drive down to the gas station and say, 'Fill it up, please. I don't want to get gas in the daytime when everyone's awake because that would make too much damn sense'."

He quotes the order of the day to the other five men on the high line detail, "Okay, everybody, no sleeping on life jackets, ten hours extra duty." The men groan at the silly order.

A whistle blows on the tanker.

"Take cover, shot-line coming over!" Jack shouts.

A pop-gun shot is heard and an aluminum missile bolt clangs around the area. Obie grabs the orange twine and pulls it until it delivers the larger messenger line. People get behind him and pull hard, bringing over the high line rope which is as thick as their wrists. The high line detail on the tanker pays-out the line faster than the destroyer team can haul it in. It sags into the waves below. The ocean drags the rope toward the churning prop wash at the stern.

"Oh shit, it's in the water. Dig-in and heave!" shouts Obie.

A tug of war begins. One man slips and falls on the salty deck and the others find it harder to pull with his weight pulling the line down. They all start sliding toward the edge of the deck. Soon they'll have to cast the line overboard to trail in the seaway beside the tanker and maybe foul her props.

Obie's grimacing. He's the first man on the line, gripping it harder than anybody but he can't stop it from paying into the sea. His foot's braced against the rail and he's squeezing the line as hard as he can. Jack sees blood on the rope where it's slipping through Obie's hands.

"We can't hold it!" shouts Jack. "Give it a turn around the lifeline stanchion if you can!"

Risking having his fingers caught and broken in the coil, Obie quickly forces a turn around the stanchion and the line stops paying out. "Good, let the tanker take in the slack," he says.

The tanker guys keep paying out the high line and the bight in the water gets longer and they're screwing-up like amateurs. It's fun to watch another ship embarrass itself. The tanker team wakes up to its problem and starts hauling slack. The high line gradually rises from the water and the destroyer crew, with arms tired from squeezing and pulling the heavy line, hauls it aboard and makes it fast to a pelican hook on the mast above their heads.

The destroyer, moving at five knots, linked by fuel hoses and ropes to the carrier, maintains a difficult one-hundred-foot separation. Fox Division pulls a canvas bag on a trolley across the high line. The bag has corners jutting out that show it contains film boxes along with mail.

"We'd better get some damn good movies out of all this work," says Obie, leaning against the bulkhead and wiping his abraded hand on his life jacket.

Jack takes the film boxes from

the bag, remarking, "Just junk, ten years old with nobody famous. The Navy's got better movies than these. Who's that stinking oiler giving the good movies to?"

"Okay," shouts the talker with sound-powered phones connected to the bridge, "Finished with high line, send it back! Bridge says next time keep the slack out'a the line."

"Shit!" says Obie, slamming his life jacket to the deck. "Stupid dumb-shit officers don't even know what a rope is and they're telling us how to handle one! That's it! I'm submitting my letter of resignation in the morning!"

The men smile and laugh. The SEMJ always works.

They sleepwalk back to their bunks or watch stations. Jack stayed on the 01 deck and watched his destroyer kick up it's heels and plow away from the sea-going gas station at full speed to impress the tanker's men with her agility. When the *Abel* was clear by two miles, she turned to starboard and resumed her northerly course.

There's nothing up there but the Tonkin Gulf, he thought. We'll probably turn east and join the task force at Point Yankee, just below western Hainan soon.

He went down to the sonar shack for his midnight-to-four-a.m. watch. They called it the mid-watch and it meant you would lose half a night's sleep and face the next workday as a zombie. The chief sonarman wasn't there. He hadn't bothered to pretend to help the workers but slept through refueling. His second-in-command, Kincaid, had the lights on and was reading a magazine. During refueling the sonar equipment is put on standby because the tanker's engines and props make too much noise to see anything on the sonar screen. Kincaid sat there anyway, rather than to go outside where the work was.

"Okay, Kincaid, I got the watch," said Jack and sat down at the sonar console. He moved switches on the stack of electronic systems to Active Search and Five Mile Range. The zinging sound of high-powered sonar pulsed into the sea could be heard through the hull. It was a sound a destroyer continually makes while underway. The men blocked it out and didn't hear it after a few pulses.

The bow line on the sonar screen indicated the ship was heading 000 true, due north.

"Does anyone know where the captain thinks we're going?" he asked Kincaid, trying to get some scuttlebutt to compensate for the official silence from above.

"To hell, if we don't mend our ways." Kincaid signed-out in the watch log and went back to bed.

The second man on the mid-watch, a Seaman, passed Kincaid in the doorway and frowned at his departing back.

"He sends the regular watch up on deck and takes it easy hanging around the shack where there's nothing to do. He's not even on the watch list, why the hell doesn't he go up to the high line detail? That fat belly would really help us pull."

"For the same reason he doesn't participate in *any* work detail, he's a lifer. If lifers would pull their load this wouldn't be a half-bad life. The minute they get a little authority the first thing they do is decide they shouldn't do any work. I'm taking it up with the morale officer in the morning." SEMJ number two: Take it up with the morale officer.

The Seaman laughed and asked, "Who's morale officer today?"

"Beats me. Pinball Wizard doesn't put unimportant stuff like that in the informative crew's newsletter referred to as 'The Orders of the Day.'

Tin Can

It's must be an undercover job. Maybe they only have them on shore stations where they have extra officers hanging around. Maybe it's only in the movies, who knows? But remember this because it'll be on your petty officer exam; Only a morale officer knows who the morale officer is."

It's hard to get to sleep after drinking coffee to stay awake on watch and your ship's on a dangerous course. You turn on the bunk light and look at a picture from a world away; Sonya in San Diego. A world where hired writers make propaganda to lull the consumers into thinking it's peacetime.

Outside in the dark, the ship rendezvous' with the "USS *Conway*," a hardy veteran World War II can that carries a spy van on its back to gather tactical electronic intelligence about radar and radio installations and operations.

They approach a northern Viet Namese military base on the island of Hon Me in the Tonkin Gulf. South Viet Namese commandos, sponsored by American spies, are sabotaging the base so its emergency military procedures can be examined by the spies inside the van on board the *Conway*. The two destroyers form an ominous artillery and surveillance umbrella enveloping Hon Me and the nearby mainland.

Back home it's three p.m. and business as usual. The government's running the war like a part-time hobby. The government is not imposing war taxes. If it did, it would have to admit there is a war. Instead it says it's engaged in a clean little conflict using high-technology, low risk weapons.

A hippie song-writer comes up with the lyrics, "You can't call it war, we're fightin'em with missiles, all you hear is whistles, don't have to see no guts nor gore."

The Treasury goes in debt and borrows battle money from the affluent classes and pays them good interest rates while it conscripts the workers' kids to do the fighting. To replenish the empty Treasury, school lunch programs and the burial allowance for veterans are reduced. Thanks for that one.

Taxes don't go up, ostrich-like citizens stick their heads in the ground and believe the conflict is affordable, just a sideline for the giant standing military force. Corporations make weapons and profits and hire every warm body in sight. Life is rich and the band plays on. Government of the people for the corporations. You don't see their sons and daughters in the ranks, they get draft deferments to go to college.

If the war isn't worth a full scale commitment by the country, what am I doing here? I just wanted to go down to the sea in ships and see the world. 'Be careful what you wish for, you just might get it,' as the saying goes. I got what I wished for, the sea and sex. Too bad they came in the form of the Navy and Sonya.

She was your first sexual girlfriend. You had been a nice boy in high school and went along with the nineteen-fifties dictum that claimed sex before marriage was depraved. You petted the adorable charms of girlfriends and stewed in your own juices. The civilized answer to sex-drive was no answer: Don't marry for sex and don't marry unless you can afford to. Tell that to your penis and tell it to pregnant Sonya. The civilized answer forced deception: Lie to girls, tell them their under-developed personalities drove you mad with a love that demanded consummation while it was actually your hormones and their well-developed bodies that drove you mad.

Tin Can

You tried it the other way and went to Chicago to buy a street girl. When you got back you told your mother, "Oh yeah mom, the museums were great." Actually, a hustler, that you hoped was a pimp, had led you to an apartment door and said, "Wait here five minutes until she's finished with another customer. She's beautiful, you're gonna like her. She'll get your rocks off real good. That'll be ten dollars commission and five dollars for a bottle of good whiskey if you want it."

Damned if you didn't order the whiskey, just to be cool. You waited outside for your woman and whiskey and finally knocked on the door. An old married couple opened it and you said, "Ah, ah, somebody must've given me the wrong address. Excuse me. Bye."

Maybe the space between school and marriage is the time that society reserves for young men to go to war. Go to war and it's okay to have sex—if you live. And especially if you win the war. Sonya had welcomed the probing of her orifices. You owed her a big favor. But your whole life?

In your bunk in a steel can on the China Sea, you wonder if you chose this life or it chose you. You semi-sleep and remember the tribulation of a young man trying to get married the night before his ship sailed to war.

Unlike California, Arizona didn't have a waiting period for marriage and so he drove there to marry Sonya on the day before his ship was to set sail across the Pacific. There was an orange sunset over the desert highway. Warm wind from the open top of the convertible played with their hair. He looked at Sonya in her white high heels with her dress pulled to the tops of her legs for coolness. Lush, fertile, inviting. In the private world of their car he put his hand on her smooth leg. She smiled and parted her thighs a little.

He lost concentration on his driving and turned off the highway onto a gravel road and found a trail and parked the car a mile from the road. She kissed him. He moved the crotch of her panties aside and put his finger there to feel the inviting warmth of her. He got out, went around the car and opened her door. She laid back on the seat and put one leg over the seat-back and the other on the dashboard and there it all was. Displayed for him and the open range, freely-offered, (he thought), what he was always wanting, complete acceptance by another human being. He lowered his pants. She saw him swollen and glistening and moved her hips in welcome. He breathed deeply in the excitement of adrenaline flow and thrust into her, actually inside a girl. The act seemed like a minor miracle. He reached for new depths and thrust until they both gasped as if speared.

"May I see some identification?" asked the Arizona Justice of the Peace.

"Do you really need that?" said Sonya. "I didn't bring any ID with me."

"I could lose my license if I married someone with no ID."

Jack explained their unique circumstances: "I'll be going overseas for three months to fight the war for you. Sonya's expecting a baby. We have to get married today or we'll have to wait until I get back. She'll be five months pregnant then."

"My license says I do everything according to law and the law says the couple must have proper ID," responded the cautious license-holder.

Sonya asked, "Won't some other form of ID be okay? How about this prescription for morning-sickness pills with my name on it? I've got a rent receipt too."

"Those are not acceptable ID's

for the purpose of marriage. Don't you have a birth certificate?"

Upset because marriage was slipping away from her and the baby, Sonya could only shake her head.

Jack took her hand and said with contempt for the man's unwillingness and her forgetfulness, "Let's get out of here, he won't help us."

Outside he said, "Let's try the Highway Patrol. If they can identify criminals they can surely identify a girl who wants to get married."

They stepped inside the Highway Patrol's small office that contained two patrolmen, a radio and a coffee pot. The second-hand of the clock on the wall ticked away the seconds remaining between the men and their retirement pensions.

"Hi, men," said Jack in a friendly, brother-in-arms way.

They didn't change. They looked at the couple who'd invaded their sanctuary. Finally the older one nodded.

"We've got to get married tonight. I'm sailing to the western Pacific tomorrow."

The senior uniform nodded again.

"The trouble is, the Justice of the Peace needs positive identification. Sonya doesn't have a driver's license. We're hoping there's some way you can identify her for the J.P."

The patrollers of highway looked at each other. "What do you want us to do?" replied the veteran policeman.

"Whatever it is you do to identify people."

"If she doesn't have a driver's license, we can't identify her."

"If she robbed a bank wouldn't you be able to identify her without a driver's license?"

"Sure we could identify her but it's got to be official business to go through all that."

"Can't you just do it because it's good? I'm a serviceman defending my country from communism and I'm only asking for one favor."

"It costs money to identify people, it's only for official business."

"How much does it cost?" asked Jack in exasperation.

"I don't know, probably more than you've got."

Jack lost his temper and picked a club from the desk and held it to Sonya, saying, "Hit him with this! He'll identify you then."

Sonya started to cry and the officers stood up, ready for action.

Jack dropped the club and said, "Don't help us," and pulled Sonya out the door. After he had the car started he yelled back, "Drink your coffee! I hope the communists get you!"

The officers were going to get mad at the impertinence but decided to laugh instead. The kid was a nut.

"Communists in Arizona. Ha-ha-ha. They feed those Navy guys real bullshit."

Driving away, he said to Sonya, "The bad thing about protecting your country is that you have to protect people like them at the same time. They ought to make everybody who wants to be defended go over and defend themselves."

He saw that Sonya felt terrible. "It's all right," he said. "We'll drive to Mexico. They'll marry anybody."

Their car's headlights were the only ones on the road to Mexico. The empty desert was black and cool and thousands of square miles of dry dirt smelled like sulfur and cow shit. She was beautiful in the faint glow of the dashboard lights. The wind moved a wisp of black hair across her forehead. She was so pretty in sleep, a sexual security blanket. Angel or whore? Life-mate or sex partner? She had been with Oberhoffen for a few months and when they broke up, Jack inherited her. Obie didn't like to be serious, didn't know how to respect women. But she was with another sailor before Obie. She's just horny, like him. That doesn't make her, or him, a whore. Should they build their sexual urges into marriage? They can try. Sweet little lost, sexy angel that he's going to help.

They got to Mexicali about eleven at night. The town was asleep except for a tourist bar in the town square.

"Let's have a drink."

"No thanks, it's too dark around here."

"I'll see if anyone can tell us where we can get married."

The bartender pointed to a house, saying, "Judge live there. He can marry you."

Jack walked to the darkened house and knocked on the door. The porch light came on and the bolt slammed open. "What do you want?" asked a gentleman in dressing gown who was struggling to control his anger.

Jack stated his predicament. The judge answered patiently, "It would mean nothing if I marry you this night. Paper of marriage must be registered in court and you no can sign paper if you no here tomorrow."

"Thank you sir. I am sorry to wake you up but I did not understand the law in Mexico."

"Da nada."

"Buena noche, judge."

Back in the car, he told her with sad finality, "I'm sorry Sonya. I tried to do the right thing but... it's just too late."

While the men are in their bunks and the ship steams through forbidden waters on the warm night, a lady named Pandora, with a fancy wooden box, flies down from the

Tin Can

Sculptor constellation and lands on *Abel*'s mast and opens the lid just enough to let her favorite demon, Chaos, escape.

"NOW GENERAL QUARTERS! GENERAL QUARTERS! ALL HANDS MAN YOUR BATTLE STATIONS FOR SURFACE ACTION! THIS IS NOT A DRILL, I REPEAT, THIS IS NOT A DRILL!"

Out of the rack, pull on dungarees and shoes, tie the laces in a flash, pull on shirt, only two buttons, do the rest later if there's time, hit the deck at a fast walk, bumping into bunks, too sleepy to run, the engines are speeding-up, this is not a drill, don't want to fall down and hurt yourself and be unable to defend the ship. Up three flights of aluminum ladders, other men scurrying up and down, clink, clink, clinking of quick footsteps on aluminum steps. Damage control parties stringing out fire hoses and shutting ventilation systems so fires can't spread, wearing helmets and fire suits, something they've never done before. Up, up, high to the bridge, hurry, bang open the steel door to the Combat Information Center, step inside, close the door, step behind your radar set. Plug in the sound phones and test them. "Gun Director 51, this is Combat Information. Sound check, over." You're either out of breath or have been hyperventilating.

You inhale deeply and slowly and calm down. "51 aye, loud and clear."

"Combat, aye. Loud and clear." That's a break, these things don't always work. You don't want to hunt around for a good set while a battle's going on. Finish buttoning your shirt and tuck it in. There's a bright wash of land only seven miles away on radar and you ask a nearby officer, "What's that?"

He looks at the blip and ignores your question. You deduce that it's an officer-level secret and that you're where you shouldn't be; seven miles from the shore of northern Viet Nam.

Combat is manned with an air of competency. The radarman with an Elvis Presley hairstyle doesn't look like a rock star now. His face is framed by earphones through which other radarmen are sending bearing and range information about some high speed surface contacts. He's calm, focused on plotting the movements of combatants on the tactical display board. Long range and darkness doesn't conceal the enemy from radar. He's drawing a surrogate battle scene that will be these men's only experience of the attack, unless, that is, one of the enemy dots gets within torpedo range and explodes the ship and this whole room descends below the surface of the ocean. That could happen but don't think about it or you won't stay calm. If you don't stay calm you can't concentrate. Do your job perfectly or die. It's that simple. This is not conflict. This is combat.

The tactical board shows a squadron of five contacts nine miles away and closing at an amazing and scary fifty knots. The room sways and lurches in the destroyer's wild flight at flank speed, about thirty knots.

The officer on the other side of your floor-mounted radar console receives instructions and points to the nearest contact and says, "Designate target one to fire control."

Your radar screen displays an electronic target hook that you can manipulate with a control stick to encircle that radar contact which appears most threatening to the ship. It's usually, but not always, the closest one. Encircling a contact causes the range-finding radar up in the gun director to home on the designated target and take an electronic aim. Its electronic aim is amplified into powerful electrical currents running servo motors in the gun mounts which aim the barrels at the target.

You snare the contact and say into the phones, "Fifty one, Combat, now designating target one."

"Fifty one, target one, aye."

Director fifty one's electronic hook moves to the blip and clings with automatic track. The gun director has acquired target and locked-on.

"Fifty one, ready to shoot."

"Good work, fire control. That you, Kaiser?"

"Kaiser, aye."

"What's happening is this. We've got five quick-boats on radar. There's another tin can out here with us that's taking the two western-most contacts and we're taking the three closer ones."

"Fifty one aye," is the terse reply from Kaiser who has work to do.

"Commence firing," says the XO, passing the order from the captain on the open bridge.

No one's heard the term before. They're not sure what to do and nothing happens.

"Are we supposed to shoot'em?" asks Kaiser incredulously over the phones.

"Wait one." You ask the ensign, "Are we supposed to shoot these contacts?" Now the ensign's doubtful. He turns around and looks at the executive officer. The XO understands the question; should a ship in peacetime be sinking the boats of another nation? He nods yes. The ensign regains his military composure and says, "You heard the order, commence firing."

"Kaiser?"

"Yes?"

"Shoot the target." That sounds better. Shooting a target is something Kaiser knows how to do from gunnery exercises. The phrase ignores death.

BANG! A shell is fired with intent to kill. Pandora chuckles.

Tin Can

Now you're in a life or death struggle. You want the shell to blow that fast boat to bits. The lives of its crew are no longer important, its lethal torpedoes are very important

BANG! The gun's recoil knocks dust from the overhead wiring. It floats in the air and shows that the radarmen haven't been cleaning their space well. You hope the shocking recoil doesn't break any of the hundreds of switches and relays that control the guns. If one tiny switch goes out, you might as well throw doughnuts at the boats because they're coming in. The reliability of electrical circuits is determining if you shall continue to live. It is not the stuff of movies where valor plays the major part. Victory goes to the best maintenance team. Dust waters your eyes. The contacts on the screen start to swim. You wipe your eyes and re-focus on the deadly blips. Every action and each second must be accomplished with near-perfection or they may become the seconds in which you die. Target one slows from fifty to five knots. Control your elation, it's too soon for cheering. You now know your guns can hit a fast boat and you may live through this.

The second target is designated. "Fifty one, Combat. Now designating target two."

"Fifty one aye. Target two."

You want to share your confidence with Kaiser and you tell him, "It looks like you damaged the first one, it's only doing five knots now."

"You expected us to miss?" is his cocky reply. Kaiser's hook moves to your hook and snares the second contact.

"Fifty one, locked on target number two and shooting," says Kaiser.

The gun crews are settling into an efficient rhythm—BANG! . . . BANG! . . . BANG! The gun circuits are proving reliable. The attacking boats may not survive.

Out in the darkness, on the windy open bridge, a phone talker reports to the captain, "Sonar reports high-speed screw noise to the north." It's an electrifying announcement. High-speed screw noise means a torpedo is in the water and running. It demands emergency evasive action, turning away from the torpedo's bearing and streaming noisemakers from the stern and firing guns into the water to decoy the torpedo's acoustic homing warhead.

The captain looks at the bearing on radar and sees an enemy boat six miles away, well out of range for launching torpedoes. "Tell sonar it's a boat six miles away and don't announce a torpedo unless it *is* a damn torpedo. Jeez." He shakes his head. Combat leadership is chaos management. The chief broke the fundamental rule of combat behavior;

don't make startling assumptions
without proof or you're encouraging
more chaos.

"Tell the chief I want to see him
after GQ. We can't have any more of
that shit."

From bow to stern, men are
doing their individual jobs without
understanding the battle. Boiler
tenders are coaxing maximum steam
pressure from the boilers, enginemen
are applying that steam to the
screaming turbines and pushing the
revolutions higher than ever before
while watching the bearing
temperatures rise. Gunners are riding
in the blasting gun mounts which are
pointed by digital information from
the gun director. The Philipino
stewards are standing-by with damage
control equipment ready to patch
battle-damage. Medics are down in the
magazines passing ammunition but
ready to go up to sick bay and patch
men who get hurt. The lives of all are

staked on the performance of each. It's an electronic arcade game played at high speed in darkness except the projectiles are lethal. The sonar chief is losing what little control he had since he heard the words "This is not a drill." His larynx tightens, making his voice squeal.

"That's torpedo noise, report it again!"

"The sonar set's useless at flank speed, chief," says the technician at the stack. "You can see that. All it's showing is noise and motorboat propellers every now and then. The bridge doesn't want to hear any more about them."

The chief descends into porcine fear and announces mightily, "A tin can sinks forty five seconds after a torpedo hits it! *Forty five seconds!* The bridge *has* to take evasive action. This is not a drill, mister, report those noises *now!*"

The talker is forced to take

personal responsibility for refusing a silly order under combat conditions and ignores the chief. One sonarman says quietly to another, "He doesn't know what's happening but he wants to run the ship. Like it ain't scary enough without his bullshit." They snort with stifled laughter.

In the urgency of a real General Quarters, the chief had buttoned his shirt in the wrong holes and half of it was hanging outside his pants. The strain of not laughing and the squealing of the chief become the funniest things in the world. The two observers involuntarily make that farting sound of laughter through noses. Chaos skulks into the room looking like the horror of death but only the chief can see him and and he becomes even more terrified.

"You guys shut up, you're on report! This is not a drill. Talker, report those torpedoes! That's it, you're on report too. It's wartime and you're both on serious report! Gimme the goddam phones, I'll report'em myself."

A tugging match begins. The talker tries to prevent the chief from getting himself into more trouble and ridiculing the sonar gang while the *Abel* is fighting for her life. Other men grapple the struggling pair to keep them from hurting each other. The chief pretends to give up. He had remembered the public address connection to the bridge.

"All right, if you pukes wanna die, it's fine by me!"

He's released. Death-fear tells him that heroic methods are needed. He switches on the bridge's loudspeaker and announces; "Bridge, sonar, the men down here are on report! I've got possible screws . . . bup, probable screws . . . torpedo screws, bearing three zero zero! Sonar recommends evasive action."

"Chief, report to sick bay,

NOW!" replies the captain.

"They don't worry up there on the bridge," says the chief. "I'm down here under the water and it's a known fact that a tin can sinks in forty five seconds. Look at that skin. That doesn't protect us from anything." He taps fearfully on the five-eighths-inch steel hull which is all that keeps the ocean outside. He raps his knuckles on it. "Half-an-inch."

BANG!!! He jerks at the gun's recoil like he sees a torpedo coming through the wall. As good as dead, he yelps and jumps away, wraps his arms around a stanchion and holds on to the steel pipe just for the sensation of existing. "I'm reporting torpedoes if I hear torpedoes, this is not a drill," he cries. He's never heard torpedoes before in his life. A stinky smell is coming from the back of his un-belted pants. They stop snickering at this eerie specter with a snapped mind.

"The captain wants you to

report to sick bay, chief," gently says the phone talker.

"The captain wants me in sick bay," he repeats and leaves the men below the waterline. "I'm going up higher, Captain's orders," he explains.

In Combat Information Center, everyone's doing well. Target one has disappeared from radar.

BANG! Another target begins to fade. Your life seems to have its future back. One contact remains bright and strong, running at fifty knots away from its dead in the water squadron, heading for land, trying to save itself to fight another day. You admire its pluck.

"Designate target three." The officer is pointing to the last live contact.

You say, "Their attack is over."

"Designate it."

Reluctantly, "Fifty one, combat. Now designating target three." The ship's been saved, the men on that quick-boat are in retreat and are no longer threats. They have lives to live and, just like you, were forced to fight because someone wrongfully ordered us into their water. Covert foreign policy gone bad.

"Fifty one, aye, target three," answers Kaiser. He lassos the runaway contact and BANG! It alters course, avoiding waterspouts from the *Abel's* detonating projectiles.

BANG—BANG! Astonishingly, its speed increases. It must've lightened ship by jettisoning its torpedoes and is coaxing every last ounce of power out of its engines.

BANG! The sea is so smooth that radar is reflecting the shot-splashes. They're short of the fleeing target. BANG! Officers and sailors are entranced by the demon vulture called Blood Lust, unleashed whenever Pandora persuades politicians to sanction the taking of human life.

BANG! The guns' recoil is

wonderful but the captain realizes he's wasting ammo. Shaking the ghoulish vulture from his shoulder, he remembers the correct phrase to stop this nonsense.

"Cease firing."

The demons rush up the mast to their box and Pandora closes the lid.

The order is passed to the gunnery stations, "Cease firing. Cease firing." The banging stops but the ship continues running southward at flank speed.

"Aren't we going to go back and pick up survivors?" you ask the ensign across the radar screen, expecting him to relay the idea to the captain. The young officer is too insecure to suggest anything to the captain. "He knows what he's doing," he says, rebuffing your enlisted man's suggestion.

"Okay," you reply, without saying 'sir.' You're still hot from battle. You imagine the satisfying feel of fisting him good in the middle of his face and sending him into the plot board. He's got poor judgment and he thinks it is his better judgment that makes him the better man.

"Yeah, leave'em there. Teach the gooks a lesson." Wising-off to these guys is the equivalent of slapping them so there's a law against it. It's called "Showing Disrespect to a Superior." You don't care. He's no Superior in any way, shape or form. He ignores your disrespect and that deflates you. You want to fight with him and go to Captain's Mast where you might be able to put your definition of the battle on an official court record: We went where we shouldn't, killed who we didn't need to, and didn't take any prisoners.

Up on the swaying mast truck, Pandora surveys the careering ship and tucks the box under her arm. The night is warm black velvet and feels like paradise. Crazy people with weapons are huge fun. She loves that

Tin Can

sonar chief who played so well without being in real danger. She smiles and stretches her blood-red wings and soars back to the jungle where a *real* storm is gathering.

SONYA

IN THE MORNING the captain radios his commodore whose flagship happens to be on liberty in Hong Kong. Being above the rules of Navy radiomen, they talk in the palsey-walsey way of old duffers on the golf course.

"How's it going Shep?" the captain asks the commodore.

"Oh, just fine, Stan. I had me an interesting little interlude with one of the local 'entertainers' last night, heh, heh, heh."

"Heh, heh. I had an interesting night myself, Shep. But probably not as exciting as yours. You'll have to tell me about it the next time we're in the Foreign Club together."

"How would you like to be there this week, Stan?"

"What an offer! I accept with alacrity."

"Well, Stan, I'm detaching your vessel from patrol duty and requesting your presence in the British Crown Colony for four days of rest and recreation. From what I hear about the fly-swatting you just did, you deserve it."

"That's a fair assumption. What're the chances for a Unit Citation Medal out of this? It'd look good on my dress whites."

"Yeah, it'd look good on mine too, now that you mention it. Did you retrieve any supporting evidence, debris or survivors?"

"Ah, no we didn't, it was a little too hairy to look for souvenirs, ha."

"How about oil slicks? See any oil slicks?"

"Shep, it was darker than the inside of a goat's ass, you couldn't even see the sea," the captain retorts nervously.

"Well, you know how the admiral is. He'll have a problem with lack of evidence. I'm sorry to say there's some sort of a... national security problem, too. Tell your boys not to talk about it."

"Okay Shep, will do. Well, I'm going to fire up the boilers and see you soon."

"Have a good trip. Liver Link out."

"Knicker Knocker out."

Tin Can

The captain looked out the bridge window for a long time. Somehow, his victory had gotten him into hot water. He deduced that gunfights arising out of covert espionage actions don't warrant medals from a grateful nation.

He turned to the conning officer, "Chart a course and speed for Hong Kong. Tell my steward I'll take breakfast in my quarters."

On a choppy gray sea, the big destroyer steamed easterly under the island of Hainan and then headed northeast toward Hong Kong. The crew was told to shut up about the battle. They weren't told why. They went about their regular maintenance in a depressed mood as the ship drove through scattered rain showers. Victory at sea dissolved in the mist.

"The XO wants to see ya. Better get up there fast," said the sonar chief to Jack, as he was scraping rust from the hedgehog mortar mount on the forward 01 deck. The chief's face was red and he was sheepish, not his old bully self.

"He's in a bad mood," said the chief. "He just cut orders sending me to shore duty. Alaska. Eighteen years of service and I get Alaska."

Jack went to the XO's stateroom and knocked with apprehension. It meant a shit ration when the XO wanted to see you in his quarters. The radar officer must have filed charges against his insubordination at general quarters.

"Yes?" came a voice from the compartment.

"Petty Officer Mason, sir."

"Come in." Pinsetter was in a cozy chair, reading mail he'd received at the last refueling. His room was decorated with wood and brass accessories. He had his own bathroom with fluffy tan towels, not the skimpy white things the men used. A brass chronometer ticked quietly on the desk.

"Mason, this letter's from the chaplain at San Diego. It concerns one Miss Sonya Detweiler, do you know her?"

"Yes sir, she's my girlfriend. Is she okay?"

"No, she is not okay. She's going to have a baby, apparently, and her family wants to know what you're going to do about it."

"I, I told her I'd marry her. We tried to get married but it was too late and I had to come over here."

The XO could've given him a hardship leave to go get married. But that would've been nice. He wasn't interested in solving a personal problem or helping Miss Detweiler, he wanted to put the pressure on somebody. He was in trouble for last night's failure to search the battle scene and he did not feel nice. Shit dribbles downward.

"Contrary to what you may think, sailors are not a bunch of studs who use women and then sail away. Letters from the chaplain go into your service record and you may very quickly find yourself facing an Unsuitability Discharge."

He gave Jack the mean eye and let more venom out of his system. "Do you think anyone's going to hire you with an Unsuitable? Do you think you can support..." he looked for a name on the papers and said, "Miss Detweiler and *your* baby on an Unsuitable?"

"No sir. I don't sir."

"You'd better take care of that girl. Here's a copy of the chaplain's letter, I want to see your written reply real soon. That is all."

Jack turned and walked across the carpet to the door with the brass knob, thinking, why can't we have carpets in our bunk room? What are we, animals?

Tin Can

Opening the door, he said "Nice carpet," boldly omitting the obsequious "sir," which should follow every statement to an officer. He quickly closed the door behind him and hastened from officers' country.

He was in the sonar berthing compartment, finishing a marriage proposal letter to Sonya, when Kaiser walked in. "Who're you writing?" he asked.

"Sonya. Pinballs said I had to marry her or get booted out on an 'Unsuitable'."

"Aw, that's the way it is around here. Everything a man does is unsuitable, undesirable, or bad conduct."

"The head chaplain in San Diego is in on it."

"What's he know about the situation? Tell him you're not the first and only guy that Sonya's ever slept with."

"Leave Sonya out of it. The baby needs a father. I think I'd like to do that."

"Damn officers telling us who to marry."

"I'm getting sick and tired of this classism. He made me feel like a ten-year-old kid up there and I'm not permitted to say anything back to his dumb ass except 'sir'. We're fighting for equality but we're working for the officer class and shooting peasants like us. What's it doing to us, Kaiser? Are we gonna be any good when we get out?"

"It's giving us guilty consciences that could ruin us for life, that's what it's doing. Ten years from now we could be at a family picnic and having a good time and then slip away and be back here, shooting the wrong people for the wrong reasons. And some of us will never come back to the party. We'll find an empty patch of desert to live in or we'll hide in bars and fantasize about being free. A bad conscience goes underground, goes into the subconscious, and the only way to make it go away is to quit saying 'They made me do it,' and to take personal responsibility for being wrong."

After a moment Jack said, "But they've got us too scared and powerless to do the right thing."

They were silent at their fate. No way out. Jack puffed a breath and slapped Kaiser on the shoulder. "Did you know Pinhole has a cabin half the size of this compartment and has his own bathroom with a bath mat that matches the towels?"

"Matching towels! Did Pin-drop ask you to take a shower with him?"

"Yes he did. He insisted I do so but I told him Sonya wouldn't have it."

Kaiser cracked up.

Obie came in and said, "You guys know where we're going?"

"Where?" they chorused. For

once, somebody knew where they were going.

"Hong Kong! Give me liberty or give me death!"

Tin Can

HONG KONG

THE GREEN HILLS OF GUANGDONG PROVINCE arise out of the sea haze and overlook warship number 907 entering Victoria Harbour. The vessel slows and stops.

Heavy chain rattles through her chain pipe and she backs both engines against the anchor like a horse testing a tether. It digs-in and holds. Safely connected to underwater ground, she extinguishes fires in three boilers and leaves one hot for running the generators and getting underway in an emergency. She cools and quietens.

Curious men go outside to gaze at the "Pearl of the Orient," Hong Kong. Cramped on a narrow shore between saltwater and steep hills, it is a world-class metropolis.

Weathered junks, with slatted black sails, catch the Asian wind and sail past the *Abel* in high contrast to her modern lines. The smell of burning charcoal and chop suey laces the humid salt air that wanders lazily over the water. Tugboats and lighters move cargoes between freighters and warehouse docks. Sampans slide over the water, propelled by one or two women who rhythmically thrust their whole bodies against the sculls, like gondoliers.

On one side of the harbor lies squalling Kowloon, Hong Kong's sister-city, with an airport that ran out of land and built a runway extending a quarter-mile into the harbor. Unseen behind the Kowloon hills is the farmland peninsula called the New Territories, covering forty square miles. That peninsula connects to mainland China, home to one-fifth of the earth's population.

"NOW HEAR THIS! MAIL CALL! ALL DIVISION PETTY OFFICERS REPORT TO THE SHIP'S OFFICE TO COLLECT MAIL. NOW MAIL CALL.

"NOW SWEEPERS, SWEEPERS, MAN YOUR BROOMS. GIVE THE SHIP A CLEAN SWEEP-DOWN FORE AND AFT.

"NOW LIBERTY CALL! LIBERTY WILL COMMENCE AT 1500 HOURS FOR DUTY SECTIONS TWO AND

THREE, TO EXPIRE ON BOARD AT 2400 HOURS. NOW LIBERTY CALL."

The liberty sections tumble into the water taxis and go ashore in a different world. Rickshaw men canter their riders around town for twenty five cents. Tiny shops on the roof-tops of the old Wanchai District sell goods and services for pennies. Tailors take days to measure, cut and sew fine suits for thirty dollars. Sexual favors of fresh young women, newly-escaped from China, are offered for five dollars. From the teeming streets, a filthy human being, so ragged that it looks neither male nor female, staggers onto the lawn of the Hong Kong Hilton with one wish; a clean place to die. The inscrutable Orient. Take it as offered.

Jack avoided the race for the gangway. Alone in the sonar bunk room, he slowly changed into his dress blue uniform and savored the prospect of liberty in Hong Kong.

Tin Can

Obie came in with a big smile. "I got a letter from Delores. You're invited to the wedding!"

"You and Dee are getting married? Great! When's it going to be?"

"Just a few months after we get back. Let's go celebrate. Come on, I'm buying."

"Ah no, not today. Let's celebrate tomorrow, I just want to walk around and look at the sights. Maybe get some civilian clothes."

"Okay." Obie's face sobered. "There's some news for you, too. Delores found a letter that Sonya was going to send to another man. Delores thinks it's something you ought'a know about. Seems like you weren't the only one Sonya was dating." He handed Jack the letter which was in Sonya's handwriting.

"Dear Dick," it started. At the end was a line that said, "I hope the baby has your wonderful sense of humor."

"Dick?! She's found somebody with a better sense of humor than me?" said Jack, trying to sound funny and unaffected.

"She's hedging her bets, Jack. She might love you but she doesn't know if you want to marry her. She wants a husband and a father for the baby. She doesn't want to go through it alone, that's all."

Jack's face started to do funny things. Obie left and closed the watertight door for privacy.

As a military man, Jack didn't know how to cry. Anger, not directed against officers, was somewhat condoned in the military but crying never was. An anguished "Ahhh" sound escaped his throat. He put a pillow against the lockers and beat them until they bent inward. He slumped to the deck with a sob and crumpled her letter and slammed it into a drawer on top of the chaplain's letter that suggested he should marry Sonya.

Jack woodenly rode the water taxi with the Chinese name "Hung Fat" to Hong Kong. He knew what hung fat felt like. Delores is marrying Obie and Sonya wants Dick. The evening sky turned red. The city lights twinkled on and echoed from the water and into his eyes and cheered him slightly.

He found a tailor shop. Upstairs, three tailors were stitching clothes by hand. They smiled and nodded whenever he looked their way. One took his measurements with full Chinese politeness. As a trained military dog, Jack was embarrassed by respect. But it felt good. He put a deposit on the suit and went back down to the streets of China. A dull ache was in his chest.

He went into a bar named "Hollywood" to get medicinal beer. There were colored dim lights and long-haired women in tight dresses.

He drank alone and looked at, but did not touch, their prettiness. After three beers the pain of Delores's engagement to Obie and Sonya's deception was fading. A bar girl with a functionary smile came over and put her hand on his back and asked his name.

"Joe."

"Hi Joe. You buy me one drink? Be good guy, okay?"

He told her to order one. He was jolted from romantic pretense when her bill was ten times the cost of his beer. A con game. After some small talk she asked, "You buy me 'nother drink?"

"No. Buy yourself drink." She went away mad and so did he.

On the streets there was a Chinaman who said, "You go upstair? Many pletty gull." He went up. Something had to shake his mood.

Upstairs was a hallway and five doors. In a seating area in the hall were three girls chatting in Chinese.

Tin Can

One stood and greeted Jack.

"You likee gull, mistah?" she said, waving toward the other two.

He was attracted to one with the short skirt and long hair. Her blouse was casually open to reveal that she neither wore, nor needed, a brassiere. Her smile was natural and looked a lot better than the girl's in the bar.

The mama-san saw approval in his eyes and said, "You go with Jasmine one half hour, twenty Hong Kong dollar."

Four bucks. A day's pay. He paid and followed Jasmine's smooth rump to her room. She looked too good for anyone to just walk in and buy. He didn't think the four dollars would buy sex with her, maybe just talking and flirting. Maybe she'd strip-tease him and demand a hundred dollars for sex, he didn't know.

He sat on the bed and said, "I Jack." She giggled at the impossibility of her pronouncing his name and just called him "Wishes" and opened her blouse.

He inhaled. She would give him all of her body, just like that. Melancholia was broken. He discarded his military facade and pulled her chest to him and became himself; a deceived boy from the firing line.

In the secret room his tears flowed onto her bosom. She understood pain, was not afraid. She helped him undress, folded his uniform and placed it on a chair. She removed her skirt and panties and got in bed. She put his hand on her mound because he was shy. She put a finger to the tip of his erection and drew a clear thread of love juice to her lips. She smiled at his surprise at the gesture. She placed a strange little Chinese pillow block under her head and pulled him over her thighs and received him deeply. When he released into Jasmine, her vagina answered with small contractions, draining him to serenity.

Later, she motioned for him to squat over a wash basin. She washed his genitals in a gesture of respect that was perhaps more intimate than sex. She washed herself over the bowl, smiling at his curious eyes.

"I can buy more time with Jasmine?" he asked.

"Yes, you tell mama-san."

When their time was ending and they lay with the world temporarily at bay, she asked him, "Where you from?"

"Kentucky."

She hadn't heard of that state. Not unusual. Largely hills and woods, there wasn't a lot there for the outside world to be interested in. No big criminals, billionaires or movies about it. Subsistence farmers, loggers, miners with silicosis, distillers, hunters and fishermen. Honest people who did fine when left alone.

"Ah, I know! Kentucky Derby.

You have horses Kentucky."

"That's right."

"We have horses Hong Kong, too."

"You lucky. Horses nice."

"You was in Viet Nam?"

"Yes, for a few days."

"What was like for you?"

She was offering to let him get rid of it but he couldn't afford enough time to explain to her his world-view on Viet Nam so he boiled it down to the simplest way he could put it. "It was like Kentucky."

Where did the tears come from? The shame of crying was okay with a secret woman he need never see again. Eyelid acid, hot as lava, rolled down his temples and pooled in his ears. What was the war good for? The National Association of Manufacturers? N.A.M. as in Viet Nam? That's where Viet Nam's resources went before, it's who's getting rich on war money right now.

Tin Can

The answer's been spelled-out for you but you'd thought it was a coincidence and too simple to be true. He had been a clown called Patriot. He owed them disgust and disobedience. His mind cleared and his tears dried. Jasmine, nude beside him, still looked too good to be true. He kissed her soft pretty breasts. Not her lips, they should be saved for love.

"Can I buy more time?" She nodded yes with a smile.

He caught a rickshaw to the water taxi dock. He admired the trotting man's endurance. His feet were bare and tough and struck the pavement lightly.

"Power," said Jack, watching the man's rhythmic legs. "Hear the power, fear the power, fear the power of fear. I pledge allegiance, to the power, and to the repugnance for which it stands. Dumb nation, under God, reprehensible, with liberty, injustice for all."

The next afternoon, Jack said to Obie as they were getting ready for liberty, "Hong Kong's too British, let's take a walk on the Kowloon side."

They caught the Star Ferry from Hong Kong to the mainland side and walked the streets of a world stranger than Hong Kong.

"All the signs are in Chinese, how're we gonna find a bar?" complained Obie.

"You don't need a sign to find a bar. Let's get some real Chinese chow first."

Seated in a restaurant, they found the menu was in Chinese. One item had a drawing of something in a bowl. They thought it might be the house special and ordered it.

"What is it?" asked Obie when it came.

"I don't know," said Jack, putting his nose to the bowl. "Smells okay."

Chinese diners in the room were watching the occidentals' odd table manners. Jack stirred the soup and looked at the morsels in the China ladle and said, "You ever see anything like this? It's like noodles, only rubbery."

Obie picked out one of the noodles and stretched it, trying to keep from laughing and said, "It's a worm."

"No, they wouldn't serve worms in restaurants. I think it might be birds' nest soup. I heard they make soup from bird snot." Obie laughed out loud at that. The Chinese were good-natured and smiled about the nonplussed Americans.

They were afraid to eat the soup. They had a few beers and went outside to walk the streets of Kowloon.

"This place is a human bee-hive," said Obie.

"God must love the Chinese because He made so many of them."

Obie looked up at the festoons of drying laundry between the buildings and said, "If God loves'em so much, why doesn't He give'em clothes dryers?"

"God doesn't make household appliances."

They came upon an incongruous cowboy-style bar and went inside. Three girls and a male bartender were at the far end of the bar jabbering in Chinese. Seeing customers, they sprang into action. The bartender played Johnny Cash songs on the jukebox and two girls ushered the sailors away from the counter and into a booth and took their orders. The women came back with beer. The older one, in a blue silk dress that was smooth against her curves, sat beside Jack. Her eyes had tiny time-lines at the corners and sparkled flirtatiously. She touched the ship's name patch on his shoulder with long pink fingernails. "What mean

Tin Can

'*Abel*'?"

He saw the way her mouth looked, symmetrical pink lips slightly smiling over ivory teeth. "Uhh . . . what?"

"What mean, *Abel*?" She did it again. Something in the way she moved her mouth. He didn't know if he was allowed to but he lightly kissed those lips and they gladly kissed back. He took a slug of beer.

"What *does Abel* mean, Obie?"

"It's the name of the brother who didn't kill his brother."

"They don't know that Bible story, what's the other definition?"

"Oh, you mean 'able.' Able means you can do something. How about you," he said, rolling his eyes at the girl beside him, "can you *do something* for me?"

Everybody laughed at the sophisticated bar talk.

"I can do something for you," Jack's girl whispered in his ear. He liked her face close and put his cheek against hers. She smelled like a million bucks.

"My name is Wong Mon Nan. Other girls jealous because I have good name."

He didn't see the good in the name but was interested in seeing it written in Chinese. He offered her a pen and a piece of paper. She wrote her name and phone number and said, "You phone me every day you in Guangdong."

He looked at her signature. It was like a sketch of boxes with legs and ribbons. "How do you say that in English?"

She laughed. "I no have English name. I Chinese, have Chinese name— Wong Mon Nan."

He wrote her name in phonetic English with nervous hands. She was terrific. The top of her dress had a row of buttons across the top and down one side. She deftly put her fingernails to work on those buttons and presented a lovely full breast, complete with an erect nipple, in front of everybody. He was a goner. They excused themselves and went to her apartment.

Her rooms seemed spacious for a Kowloon bar girl, if that's all she was. She turned on the stereo, lit two candles and said, "Take off shoes, lie down in bedroom. I get some brandy."

I'm going to get it all, here in a Kowloon boudoir with a gorgeous, well-built woman that I just met an hour ago. She probably thinks I've got a lot of money to offer.

In high heels and loose kimono, she came into the bedroom with crystal glasses of brandy. She bent to place the glasses on the bedside table and her robe fell open and displayed her charms to him. Her curly triangle, soon to be his, made his adrenaline pump. Too fast, too surreal in the candle light.

"Wong Mon Nan, you lovely woman but I no have much money."

"I don't need money. I like you."

"I like you too. You're fascinating."

She didn't understand.

"Fascinating means very wonderful."

She laughed merrily and un-did the thirteen buttons on his dress blue trousers. He again looked for a trick to his good fortune cookie.

"Why you so good to me?"

"You handsome young man, have good body. How many girl you have before me?"

"Two."

"Ah, two," she said, smiling at his youth. "You cherry man."

She took his bursting almost-cherry in her mouth and surreality closed-in and was fine.

On his next liberty day she took him on a drive through the New

Tin Can

Territories. He discovered Hong Kong was not just a metropolitan seaport but a thousand-square-kilometer pocket nation.

She shouted "Ting hai!" as she waved to a truck driver who had slowed-down and driven close to the road's shoulder to let her pass in her little English roadster.

"What mean 'ting hai'?" asked Jack.

"Ting hai mean good," she said.

"Wong Mon Nan ting hai," he said, trying to say a whole sentence in Chinese. She was happy with his effort and ruffled his hair.

"How you get rich, Nan?"

"I number-one business girl for American corporation. When they have customer in Hong Kong they call me. One customer, he love me very much, he buy me car. Buy me apartment, too. He work for National Assosayshun of Manufacture. You know that company?"

"Do I? I work for it too." He smiled to show her it was a joke and she knew from his uniform that he didn't work for civilian lobbyists. She was delighted by his joking, whatever it meant.

"He old, I no love him," she added to reassure Jack that she was not mentally in bed with slavers, that today her affection was his alone.

They approached a gray blockhouse that controlled a swinging gate across the road. Nan slowed and parked.

"There China."

He gazed at the coastal plain of Asia. Beyond the gate was China with Russia beyond, countries that supposedly were responsible for the falling capitalist dominos of the world. His warship, twenty miles away, would never dare to fire on this big dragon. Better to shoot peasants in some rice-pot country that doesn't even have a Navy or Air Force.

"It's big," he said with futility.

She looked him in the eyes and said, "You nice man, you gonna be all right."

Coming from one such as her, he felt it might be true.

A communist guard came out of the blockhouse and stared sullenly at them, making Jack uncomfortable without a warship supporting him.

"Let's go back, I want to taste your brandy again."

She kissed him in the sunlight of the good side of the border and he felt love, in a liberty-call sort of way.

The display of a Chinese female preferring a western male made the guard take the rifle from his shoulder and hold it threateningly in front of him.

"Ting hai!" he shouted to the soldier and jumped in the white sports car and they drove away.

STOCKADE

REST AND RECREATION IN HONG KONG ENDED after four days. The anchor winch whined powerfully and took a strain on the chain. The links filed up from the bay, across the foredeck and down into the chain locker. The *Abel* cleared Victoria Harbour and took the Tat Hong Channel to deep water. When she was out on the rolling blue again, her bow swung around to the southwest.

Crew members who could tell direction knew she was returning to Viet Nam. That's when Torpedoman's Mate Oberhoffen took some food, water, drugs, and a bucket for a toilet and locked himself inside the torpedo shack. He didn't come out for muster or chow or watches. The Navy could take a flying leap at a rolling doughnut for all he cared. He was on strike.

Ship's routine tried to proceed as usual but couldn't. Too much weirdness was in the air. One warship guy had just said "No" to the captain, "No" to the Navy and "No" to the government for which they stand. That Obie was conducting a one-man war-protest on board a warship in a war zone was far too brazen for the intimidated crew to understand.

"He's freaked-out on drugs," went the scuttlebutt. That was the officers' standpoint. How could anyone in his right mind not be thankful for military conflict? Military conflict justifies huge budgets for armed forces and means impressive combat entries in service records and promotions and bigger pensions. Anyone who prefers morals to money has to be on drugs.

"A person will say and do anything when they're on drugs," they pronounced and nodded to each other.

The chief torpedoman from Alabama was on the sound-powered phones and talking to Obie in the torpedo shack. "When'ya comin' outa there, Obie? I gotta get my tools out and do some work. I'm tired of standin' around all day."

"That's all you ever do, you lazy lifer! Why's it bother you today?" His face was haggard in the dim light. "Hey chief, you wanna smoke some dope? I got some good shit from Cambodia, no Agent Orange in it."

"Yeah, let me try some of that stuff."

"Bullshit. Get me Guns, the gunnery officer. I don't want to smoke dope with you, I don't even want to talk to your dumb lifer hill-billy ass."

The chief growled back, "You're comin outa there if I hafta get a 'cetylene torch and cut your ass out."

"I see one spark in here and I'm setting-off this warhead and I'm blowing the whole damn side out of the ship! Now stick your torch up your cornhole! Get me Guns on the phone."

To a signalman on the bridge he shouted, "He wants to talk to Lieutenant Johanson!"

The officer came down, took the phones and asked, "What's the matter Obie? What can I do for you?"

"You know what murder is, Guns? You're in charge of the battery, you've been to war college, surely you know what murder is."

"I don't know, Obie. I guess murder depends on the circumstances —how you look at it."

"Exactly! Killing people when there's no war is murder. Killing people who ain't bothering you is murder." His voice went wet and slobbery. "Killing people who can't shoot back is murder. Killing people who just want us to go away is murder." His voice faded into self-pity. "Well, I ain't going to do it no more. You can't make me." He said it like a child and cried and made sobbing noises into the mouthpiece.

The officer swallowed his disgust and replied. "I'm sure there are valid reasons for shore bombardment. We've got a conflict to win."

"There ain't no damn conflict in Viet Nam! There ain't no enemy in Viet Nam except us!"

The officer was silent. Humpty Dumpty time. Obie had committed two cardinal military sins: believing the truth and acting against lies. He was useless. The Navy wouldn't even want him scrubbing pots in the scullery behind the mess hall in the dark at Adak, Alaska. He can't be put back together again.

"What do you want me to do, Obie?"

"Take the ship out of action. We're not going back to Viet Nam."

"Okay, I'll see what I can do. Maybe they'll change our sailing orders. You just take it easy in there. Gunnery out."

"Torpedo shack out," Obie replied, correctly, from phone talker habit. Change sailing orders. Guns really believed he was nuts. He took a full deep breath and said to himself, "Medical Discharge, here I come."

Every workplace and General Quarters station on the *Abel* had a sound-powered phone outlet nearby. The warship was designed so its crew could talk to each other from every part of the ship even if electrical power was lost. All the phone wires had junctions in a compartment below the mess deck called Internal Communications Central. Here, phone circuits could be re-routed in case of battle damage to any circuit.

IC technician Starkey was the shipboard version of the old country switchboard operator who could listen at will to any conversation on the network. He looked like a technical cowboy with tools and meters dangling from a heavy work belt slung low around his hips and he wore his white hat low on his forehead, just below his eyebrows. He had just summoned Obie's friends down to IC Central so they could hear an incredible conversation taking place on the ship's phones. Starkey had patched the torpedo shack's phone line into a loudspeaker so that Kaiser, Val Scarputti and Jack could overhear the dialog between Obie and Guns.

"The enemy is us... Take the ship out of action..." Obie was saying.

"He's right. I wish we could help him," said Kaiser.

"We'd have to steal the ship to help him now," said Jack. "He's gone too far, said too much. He's sunk."

"Isn't there another way to help?" asked Kaiser.

"Well, everybody else could get high on drugs and lock themselves in. That would make Obie look better," said Scarputti, enjoying the fantasy.

"No, we'd get the big DD, Dishonorable Discharge. Civilians don't hire you with one of those," said Starkey.

"Maybe they'd just give us Medical Discharges," said Jack.

Starkey replied, "One guy can get a Medical but if everybody tries it they start handing out Dishonorables. You're only allowed one Medical per ship, says so in the UCMJ."

"Well, what about this," replied Jack with mock drama. "We go for all-out mutiny. We lock the officers in the wardroom at chow time. We tell them they can have the ship back if they let Obie go and don't press charges against us."

"Yeah," said Kaiser, excited by the game. "We can promise not to tell the hippies and the news media and the anti-war movement back home that there's been a mutiny aboard a United States Navy warship. Ha-haa! I bet'cha they'd have let us go!"

"Right! And we could lock the chiefs in their lounge. Starkey here could disconnect the phones so they couldn't talk to each other" offered Scarputti.

Starkey the engineer smiled at his part in the play. "Yeah, and I'd cut off their water so they couldn't drain the tanks and I'd shut down their power so they couldn't short out the generators. I'd block'em off tighter'n a drum."

"And what would we do with all the men who didn't want to go with us?" said Jack in fun.

"Same deal," said the engineer. "Lock'em in the mess deck at chow time. Put a gun on'em and tell'em to decide whose side they're on."

"Fletcher Christian put them in a gig and pushed them off," mused Jack.

"Wish we had a bigger gig," said Scarputti.

"That's the problem, getting rid of the lifers and the zombies." Kaiser offered, "We could let them off in Danang, it's close. Then we could find a neutral country to take the ship to and ask for political asylum."

"Then we could sneak off to Hong Kong and hide for seven years until the statute of limitations runs out!" suggested Jack enthusiastically.

Kaiser laughed. "We oughta keep some officers on board as

hostages so the Navy won't blow us out of the water."

"We'd have to put the crew off," Jack replied. "There's too many of them to watch all the time. We'd keep a few officers for insurance and we'd take the ship out of action, just like Obie said, just like he wants."

"What countries are neutral?" asked Kaiser.

"Beats me. I'm not sure any country's neutral."

"Why not go straight to Hong Kong?" asked Kaiser.

"Nah, it's an English colony and the English hate mutineers with a passion. Did you know they tracked the mutineers of the "HMS Bounty" all the way to Pitcairn Island twenty years later and took them back to England and hung them? They'd hang us for free."

"Northern Viet Nam then."

"No! They're too mad at us. They'd take the ship and use it against our sailors and torture us for being Americans."

"How about Red China?"

Jack thought. "The Red Menace? You'd give the ship to the Red Tide, as it's called in National Geographic and Readers' Digest? Oh, the Navy would very much not like that. They might start a military conflict with China if it did not give the ship back. I think we should go to a neutral country."

Kaiser offered, "Maybe officers are allowed to know politics. One of them might know who's neutral."

"Maybe. Kaiser, you know Guns pretty well, why don't you ask him?"

"Yeah, I could try. I don't think he'd report me for asking political questions." Kaiser had a dampening thought, "What if he says nobody's neutral?"

"Then we can't take the ship. Where would we take it? Out to sea until the food runs out? We need someplace to go. But I wouldn't worry, there're probably dozens of countries that would love to get their hands on a new general purpose can with a fully trained crew, even *if* that crew is a little . . . shall we say, rebellious?"

They laughed at their imaginary revenge on the Navy for destroying Obie. They adjourned and went to get some sleep, a commodity of which they'd had too little in Hong Kong.

"NOW SET THE SPECIAL SEA DETAIL FOR HIGHLINE PERSONNEL TRANSFER!"

They went to their high line stations on the 01 deck and found the ship approaching an aircraft carrier from astern. In five minutes the *Abel* was alongside the floating airport. Shot lines, messenger lines, fuel hoses and high line were connected between the two ships. A personnel transfer chair was sent over from the carrier and dangled at the destroyer's end of the rope like a gallows noose. The master at arms appeared with a sidearm strapped to his waist and carrying Obie's Sea bag. He drew his .45 and rapped it on the torpedo shack door. "Carrier's here, time to go!" he shouted through the steel.

The six handles of the watertight door opened one by one and Oberhoffen stepped out. He had given up. Unshaven and gray, he looked beaten.

He turned his face away from the guard and shouted to Jack and the highline team, "Are you guys ready to go home?" And giving a huge smile: "The captain's agreed to leave Viet Nam!" Then he gave a few big winks to show that his sane self knew the captain was lying.

He moved to the aluminum transfer chair under the red night-light on the mast and sat down. The chair was hoisted and heaved across the gulf toward the floating airport which had a detachment of Marines to protect its officers and run its brig. Obie stood up and hollered, "Piss on all you dumb lifers!" He opened his fly and pissed in the seaway as he was being hauled away.

"Good exit," said Kaiser. "I think he'll get his Medical."

The Navy, being a god of war, is a vengeful god. Obie's mutiny was over. Now began the Navy's grinding-up and spitting-out process. Obie would get a discharge but they wanted us to know that getting out was harder than getting in. Harder than just taking drugs and isolating yourself. You had to pay handsomely to terminate your servitude. Officers could submit a resignation and quit for free but enlisted men were trapped.

Obie's bouncing hi-line chair moved toward the carrier's hangar deck, illuminated in the lava-red night lights like the calderas of Hell. Below him was the seaway, chopping and foaming against the slow-moving ships. He could jump and swim to freedom, maybe. But he didn't know where land was. At least he could screw-up the operation, add more points to his craziness score. The destroyer would have to unbuckle from the carrier, search for him in the dark, lower the whaleboat if they found him and fish him out and ask the carrier for another rendezvous. The carrier probably wouldn't wait around for one sailor, it had a war to conduct and planes to launch. He let his last chance pass. He arrived at the lowered aircraft elevator which was used as a work platform for the carrier's high line detail. The hi-line slackened and lowered him to the deck.

"Hello, boys," he said, like a special visitor. The line-handlers held the chair and motioned for him to get out. A Marine enlisted man stepped forward with a set of handcuffs and asked, "Petty officer Oberhoffen?"

"That's me. Are you the

reception committee?" He tried to set a pleasant tone for his incarceration and let everybody do their jobs calmly. But the Marine was trained otherwise. His iron voice barked, "About FACE! Hands behind your back!"

Obie's former shipmates watched the performance from thirty yards away. Obie turned around, put his hands, hands that had done so much for the ship, behind his back. Handcuffs flashed and locked his wrists. The charade of benevolent dictatorship was over. He was now under the command of direct physical abuse.

"Put your condom on, pecker-head," said the Marine jailer, removing Obie's white hat, turning it inside out and cramming it down over his head and eyes like a canvas bucket. He gripped Obie's collar and marched him into the darkness of the giant ship.

Third Class Torpedoman Oberhoffen was no longer a fighting

bluejacket, he had become meat for the slaughterhouse.

The *Abel*'s captain was talking over the radio to his boss on the carrier. "Yeah, Shep, thanks for taking that bad apple out of my barrel. You know, he was a bad example for the rest of the boys, they kind of looked up to him. Maybe you should make an example out of him. The Army Stockade wouldn't be too good for his kind. Do you think you could pull off something like that, in all your glory?"

"Umm, yeah, I think we might be able to swing it."

"What Shep wants, Shep gets. I owe you one. If there's anything I can do, just say the word."

"Just keep kicking butt on those mosquitoes up in the Gulf."

"Will do, with pleasure."

Marching to the carrier's brig, with his hat pushed down to the end of his nose, Obie could see only his shoes. He was ordered to halt beside a locked steel door.

"Head against the bulkhead, feet back and apart," said the guard as he pushed Obie's head hard against the bulkhead.

"Feet back and apart!" repeated the guard as he clicked the club against Obie's ankle bones.

"OW" said Obie, moving his feet quickly.

"Don't say 'ow'," said the guard, clubbing the arch of Obie's foot.

"OWW!" said Obie with emphasis. His feet were kicked out from under him and his full weight fell on his shoulder and face. A heavy knee bore into his back and made him groan.

"You will not moan unless I order you to moan. Is that clear?"

"Clear," grunted Obie.

"Clear what?" asked the guard.

"Clear as pie," answered Obie in pain.

A harder tap on the head.

Tin Can

"'Clear, SIR is the correct response."

In pain but sane, Obie grunted, "Get off me, you fool. You don't outrank me. You ain't no damn 'sir'."

The physical assault stopped. The knee got off his back. "Oh goody, I got me a live one. I got me a sea-lawyer who knows who is and who isn't a sir. Son, I'm not going to put you in the nasty old brig, I've got an even better place for people like you. C'mon now, get along little doggie."

Obie struggled to get to his knees but his hands were behind his back and his head was ringing like a red-hot bell.

"Get up." The guard thwacked him a good one across the butt. "Get up." The guard struck hard at each calf muscle. Obie quit trying to rise. He was lifted to his feet by his collar, gagging, and was marched, dizzy and nauseous, to the special place for trouble-makers, the anchor chain compartment up in the very bow of the ship.

"Where are you taking me?" said Obie, as if it were his right to know his whereabouts.

"Now listen up. I'm going to give you one simple order. No, make that two simple orders. Shut up and *stay* shut up."

The guard unlocked a small rusty door and took the cuffs off Obie. "Get in." He pushed Obie over the coaming to fall on his forehead against heavy chain. His head was like an empty, burning, broken eggshell and it went to sleep.

When he came to, hours later, he tried to escape his world of hurt by filling his mind with images from the natural world. Catfishing on the Missouri. Driving through open miles of wheated prairie. Picnics with pretty girls. Warm sunlight, summer days. He did as the guards demanded, let them hurt his body without response. He knew it would either survive or not survive, what good's worrying going to do? The pain was there but the mind could fly.

He worked on a project to exercise his muscles. He moved the heavy links inch by inch in the darkness and put a half hitch in the chain that would prevent it from paying out through the chain pipe when the big ship tried to lower its anchor. He previewed the image of some pompous captain hollering down from the bridge of his majestic aircraft carrier, "What's taking so long to lower the anchor?" "It's stuck sir. It won't go down," replies the frustrated chief bosun.

"Ahh-ha-ha-haa." Obie laughed in the black room. Steel bulkheads reverberated his humor. Pain transcended.

"There's a sailor down here," he shouted. "If there's any way to do something, a sailor will find it!"

After a few days he was taken to

sick bay and his wounds were cleaned. He was taken to a shower and given clean dungarees, then marched to the flight deck.

Scared flight deck crew looked at him, knowing it could happen to them. Scuttlebutt had it he took drugs. Most of them were interested in trying drugs. It was the sixties. The example was having the wrong effect. They kind of admired his bravery and considered getting caught his only offense.

Because he had taken drugs, the Navy put a helicopter at his disposal. Before, they'd only given him twenty-five dollars a week and a clothing allowance, fifty dollars a year. The smallest requests had to be written down so they could be officially refused by every misanthropic link in his chain of command. He laughed at the Navy's supplying him with a private aircraft.

The air crew looked grimly at each other. They were in the presence of a crazy man and they knew it could happen to them if they disobeyed orders. They often wanted to disobey orders. They were why the Navy went to so much trouble to punish its ocean of obedient little people, all obeying, always obeying, like tides in the ocean, without question or conscience. When a little person became disobedient he was turned into a walking dead person, like Obie.

"Arghh, I'm a dead man," said Obie out loud and chuckled.

The pilot went off-course under Obie's effect. Obie couldn't be stripped of power.

The truck-driver at the airport loaded the prisoner detail for The Stockade where the specters of broken prisoners made him feel like he was driving through a living cemetery. The driver noticed one man in the detail who wore blue denim trousers from the sea. Must be Navy. Don't see many of them here. Humble, passive, proud, walking with the hint of a rolling deck under his feet. Good to see someone standing tall.

Obie saw respect in the driver's eyes and gave him a joke. "Argh, I be a scurvy mutineer, I be!"

The driver loved it. The colonel could piss up a rope if he thought he was going to break this guy.

The truck drove through the chain-link gates. A latrine detail was at work and black fumes of burning shit snaked though the compound. The sun glinted off Conex shipping containers, shiny steel ovens giving the jail the nickname of Silver City.

To scare men into fighting, there has to be something worse than combat. This was it. It's commander wasn't just keeping the men, he was breaking them. A naked and sweating man was in each Conex. Obie recognized their faces as American.

"Hey. Hey! Those guys are us!

Tin Can

Those guys are Americans!" Obie expected his guard to do something about the great mistake.

"Shut the hell up! They're prisoners," said the guard.

"Wahh!" Obie screamed and lost control at the display of military hatred for its own men. "Wahh! You sonsa bitches. You sonsa bitches!" He let the rage flow. He screamed at the horror, kicking the door and venting his utter disgust overtly at last. The guard clubbed him and put him to sleep.

No senses . . . No reality . . . Confinement. Wooden box, too small to straighten-out. Voices along a corridor... "Box ten requests permission to use the head, SIR!" "Box two requests permission to use the head, SIR!" No connection to known experience. Is this a vast latrine where people have to ask to take a shit? An image of a painting by Hieronymus Bosch depicting the horrors of hell?

Doo-doo falling out of their asses and dropping on creatures already miserable from too much indecency; eyes pecked-out by storks, limbs cut-off by axes. Blood in their mouths, permanent grimaces. He huddles in a ball so the shit and the clubs and the blood roll off his body. He sleeps but even there, dreams of more hell.

That evening, Lieutenant Johanson, Guns, was sitting on the gun director and looking at the sky. Kaiser, testing circuits inside the director, knew Johanson was disturbed. Officers were never seen looking at the sky. Poor military bearing, bad for careers. Only Johanson kept his perspective. Still, his promotions came faster than the others'. He wasn't a robot, he was what the others were trying to be, competent and modest without offering their own pride as a burnt offering to authority. Kaiser stepped out of the director and asked up to Johanson, "What'cha lookin' at?"

"Orion. The Hunter."

"Where's it at?" "Up there, see those three stars in a row?"

"Uh-huh."

"That's his belt. The two big stars below are his knees and the two big ones above the belt are his shoulders. Betelgeuse and Bellatrix"

"Oh, I see. Orion."

"The curved line of stars on his right side are his bow. It's pointed at that big orange star in Taurus called Aldebaran, the eye of the bull, a main navigational star."

"I've always wondered about that. How do we navigate by stars?"

Johanson chuckled. "It took centuries to figure out and you just ask, 'How do we do it?' "

"No, I just mean basically. It's not like I want to navigate the ship tomorrow." He smiled a secret smile.

"All right, look at it this way. If

the earth weren't spinning around, if it were perfectly motionless, the stars wouldn't move at all, would they?"

"Right. They'd stay in the same place forever."

"Okay. Then every place on earth would have a star directly overhead that never moved, right?"

"Right."

"So if Aldebaran were the star that stayed directly over Hong Kong, what would you do if you wanted to go to Hong Kong?"

"I'd find Aldebaran and head for it and when I was right under it, I'd be in Hong Kong."

"By George, I think he's got it. You couldn't be anywhere else."

"Ah. Then why is celestial navigation so hard?"

"Time. Time moves things around and changes everything. What used to be true becomes false and you need math to figure out what went wrong. It's difficult for some."

After a moment Kaiser asked, "Do you think there's a right and wrong to everything but most people aren't smart enough to figure the real issue?"

"That's sort of what I just said, isn't it?"

"Lieutenant Johanson, if you don't mind my asking sir, why'd we go into the gulf?"

The officer balked. "Politics is taboo aboard ship."

"Yeah but I could've lost my ass back there. I'd kind of like to know why."

"Fair question, up to a point. We're paid to 'risk our asses,' as you put it and it's the politicians' job to decide where to send them."

"Why'd they send them to the gulf?"

"They wanted to see if the conflict had scared Hanoi enough to allow us in the gulf."

"What difference does it make

whether we can get in the gulf or not?"

"It's supposed to be international waters with free access. If they don't let us in, it's an act of war. No, it's not war. It's more like . . . political conflict."

"So we keep on doing what we're doing, for politics?"

"See that group of stars in Taurus? That's the Pleiades. Young, hot stars. We don't use them for navigation. Do you want to learn about stars or don't you?"

"Sure, I like the stars. But is there any country neutral, one that doesn't take sides in the war?"

"It is not a war. If it were, China would get involved."

"I'm sorry, that's right, it is not a war, it's a conflict, I forgot. Is there any country that's totally neutral about this, ah, conflict?"

"Cambodia, damn it. G'night!" said Johanson and left.

Tin Can

Jack was taking instrument readings in the sonar generator room when Kaiser came in with Gunners Mate Goodwin and said, "Cambodia's neutral and it isn't far away, we could get there on one tank of gas."

"Cambodia? Who told you Cambodia's neutral?"

"Guns just told me."

"I don't know where he's been getting his information but Cambodia is not neutral. I've talked to Marines that've been stationed there. They said they wore civvies so no one could tell who they were and they painted-out all the US insignia on their equipment."

"Well, it's supposed to be neutral. Guns doesn't lie."

"What a country is supposed to be, and what it is, are two big and different things. Haven't you learned that by now, for Chrissake? Look at your own country! Forget about it. We can't take the ship anywhere. Game over. It was fun for a while but now it's over. In three months we'll be home and this war will be someone else's problem."

"I don't want three more months of this crap." There was dribble at the sides of his mouth. Jack hadn't realized till now the depth of Kaiser's aversion. "I'm not killing one more person if I can help it. We could still take the ship to China."

"You realize, do you really realize, what that means?"

"Damn right I realize! I realize that Viet Nam's defending itself against everything we can throw at it. I realize that the ship's on the wrong side. I don't want to be on the wrong side any more. That's what I realize."

Goodwin spoke with a growly voice, "That's right. That's enough of this shit." He was not verbose and he knew his mind all the better for that.

The three powerless sailors sat in the steel gray room in such silence that the air blowers and waves against the hull became audible.

Jack made the final argument. "We are clean, comfortable and reasonably secure inside a war zone. We have bright futures in industry and families to look forward to. All we have to do is kill the wrong people and forget about it. That's all we gotta do."

"You want to try to forget about it for the rest of your life?" asked Goodwin.

"No."

"Me neither."

Kaiser said, "We'll be front page news but what else can we do? There's no way to resign without dishonoring ourselves like Obie did. Let's get some small arms, lock up the lifers and get the ship outa here."

"We'd have to wait till tomorrow when everyone's at chow. We'd need some engineers and boiler tenders," said Goodwin.

"Starkey's with us," said Kaiser, "He knows which engineers to get.

Goodwin can get us weapons from the small arms locker. You think we could run the ship without officers?"

"No," said Jack. "We'd get lost. Kaiser, just who the hell do you think runs the ship *now?*"

"Okay," said Kaiser, relieved and light-hearted again. "Okay. Whee-hoo! Going to China! The only country the government won't mess with."

Tin Can

HAINAN

THE MUTINY STARTS at 1730 hours
in the ship's control center, the bridge.
Jack, Goodwin and the accomplices
are up there loitering like they're

taking in the sea view when all the electrical power goes off.

The Officer of the Deck looks around in bewilderment. Goodwin steps up against him and says, "It's all right, it's just a mutiny," and pins his arms behind his back and handcuffs him and says, "Now let's go down to the wardroom, all your friends will be there."

Accomplices conduct the five enlisted bridge watch-standers down the stairs and to the mess deck.

Jack passes an order over the 1MC : "NOW HEAR THIS! EMERGENCY! ALL HANDS ASSEMBLE IN THE MESSDECK. EMERGENCY. ALL OFFDUTY PERSONNEL AND ALL NON-ESSENTIAL WATCH-STANDERS ASSEMBLE IN THE MESS DECK IMMEDIATELY. I REPEAT, THIS IS AN EMERGENCY CONCERNING THE SHIP'S SAFETY. REPORT TO THE MESSDECK. THIS IS NOT A

DRILL."

When he hears the announcement, Kaiser crosses himself for good luck, takes a deep breath and closes and locks the wardroom doors and cuts power to the compartment. Val does the same thing to the chiefs' lounge.

The crew hastens from their racks and tumbles into the mess deck which is manned by men with side arms. Jack comes down from the bridge and stands with Kaiser and Starkey at one end of the room.

"The ship's got a special emergency taking place!" shouts Jack. "Everybody come in and listen up! LISTEN UP! We're taking over the ship! We don't believe this war is worth a shit and we're doing something about it. All those who feel the same way, step over here!"

The engineers that Starkey has enlisted move out of the group to Jack's side. He gives them side arms and sends them down to the engineering spaces to keep the ship running and send up any watch-standers who are loyal to the war.

The men are aghast at suddenly being told to think big and think for themselves. They know it's seriously illegal and most couldn't do it to save their lives, much less to save their spirits, even if they had any.

Some of them eye the door and begin edging toward it.

"Excuse me!" says Jack, cocking the slide on his .45. The bolts of the rifles of the other mutineers are heard cocking, too.

"Do NOT move around. You are safe only if you do not move around. The penalties for moving around are extremely high, more than you could bear.

"Now hear this and hear it well! We're going to negotiate for safe conduct back to the States in exchange for keeping this . . . this, well, mutiny is what it is, out of the newspapers. We think the military will grant us safe conduct in order to avoid extremely bad publicity about this half-assed war. That's the deal. Now you can either ante-up or sit this one out. All those in favor, step over here. All those opposed, stay over there. You finally have to really decide, put your money on one and let the other one ride."

Only twelve men value their consciences above their security and leave the herd to save themselves through mutiny.

"Wait for me on the bridge," Jack tells them. "We'll let the rest you off the ship in two hours, then we're heading for political asylum in neutral Cambodia," he strategically lies.

He follows the other mutineers out and locks the doors behind him.

Up on the bridge, the mutineers are excited. Men are rushing into the room, slamming the door and speculating on what to do next.

Kaiser is stuttering and drops his pistol, which could've killed somebody if it went off. Jack observes the men and shakes his head in disgust that they're losing control of themselves.

"Steer due east," he says to the helmsman.

"Due east, aye sir."

"Knock-off that 'sir' stuff."

The helmsman smiles. "Due east, aye."

"Now quiet!" he shouts to the milling men. "This is a state of war! We've gonna have every ship and plane in the US Navy looking for us and we're gonna be at General Quarters until this thing's over!"

The men quiet down. A rhythmic banging becomes audible through the ship's hull; bang bang boom.

"What's that?"

"It's them," answers Jack, "doing the only thing they can do, beating bulkheads and stomping the deck." "We'll take care of them in a minute. Right now we've got business to discuss. From now on, the Navy's gonna be after us night and day. We're going to be at constant GQ. Remember how good you were in the Tonkin Gulf and stay like that until this thing ends. Val, tell the men what our strategy is."

Val turns away from the chart of the China Sea he'd been studying and says with assurance, "This mutiny can, and actually *should*, succeed. The *Abel* is a roving knight with unique moves which the Navy cannot duplicate. Moves such as sailing through Chinese waters. Our first advantage is that they don't know where we're going. We are not going to Cambodia like Jack told the zombies. Our second advantage is that even if they did know where we're going, they couldn't follow. We're going through the Tonkin Gulf to Canton, China. Not Canton, Ohio. Not Canton Atoll in the Phoenix Islands.

We're going to Canton, China."

The men are incredulous.

"The US is afraid of China and they think we are too. But we'll be in Chinese water all the way."

"Steer due north," says Jack to the helmsman, "We're going back into the Tonkin Gulf. What's our speed?"

"Thirty one knots," answers the helmsman.

"Good. We'll be at Hainan in... five hours. We'll get close to shore, lower the gig and drop the men over the side with life jackets. The gig can pull them all to shore on a long swimmers' towline."

"Aren't we going to let them get their stuff out of their lockers?" asks Kaiser.

"No we are not," answers Jack. "That would be a courtesy and a breach of security to let them rummage around the ship. Do you want to be courteous to those guys, listen to them!"

Tin Can

Bang bang BOOM!

"All they want is our ass in a sling. The smallest mistake will put us in checkmate, as Val would say. Serious, maybe firing squad, checkmate We've got to do everything as perfectly as we can. You want to spend fifty years in federal prison just so the lifers can have their spit kits?"

Bang bang Boom!

"Starkey, go break-out a wardroom porthole and put a fire hose on those guys. Then wedge a twelve-foot fog applicator into the overhead so they have a problem to work on. Show them that this ain't no fraternity party, would you please?"

"Understood," says Starkey.

Bang bang BOOM!

Jack continues: "Val is our strategist. What he says goes without question. Anyone disagrees, put on a life jacket and leave the ship, it's that simple. This mutiny is not going to be run by committee. Val, what did you say about our obstacle to success, dissension in the ranks?"

The banging in the ship's hull changes to mere shouting and then the prisoners quiet down.

"That's better. Val, you were saying?"

"We can't have one ounce of disagreement. We're at skeleton strength. If one man doesn't go along with the program, he'll break our advance and put us in checkmate."

"Everybody understand?" says Jack. "No mistakes and no Mister Nice Guy because that's how we're going to operate from now on. Repeat after me! No mistakes and no Mr. Nice Guy!"

"No mistakes and no Mr. Nice Guy," they say quietly.

"Louder! This is your order of the day! No mistakes and no Mr. Nice Guy!"

"No mistakes and no Mr. Nice Guy! No mistakes and no Mr. Nice Guy!"

Tin Can

"All right! Hainan in five hours, then it's Swim Call for lifers!"

At 2045 hours the ship slows to a halt. The lights of Gancheng village are showing faintly on the dark shoreline of the Chinese island of Hainan. The gig is lowered and a rope with a buoy at the end is tied to the stern. Armed mutineers open the doors to the dark mess deck and file the loyalists out. Goodwin watches as they each take a life jacket from a pile.

"Keep moving! Put them on in the water! Go!" he orders.

Some giggle and balk at the rail as they don their jackets.

"Get your asses in gear! This ain't no bullshit picnic!"

BAMBAM! Goodwin fires two authoritative shots into the air and the men respond by rapidly leaping into the sea.

Goodwin pulls a friend out of the line and says to him: "Jake, I know you'd be with us if you weren't so close to retirement. Can I trust you to give this to the Chinese authorities without letting anyone see what you're doing?"

Jake looks at Goodwin's waterproof envelope quizzically. "It's a letter telling the Chinese that we're sailing for political asylum in Canton and why. You'll sink my ass if you let the captain get ahold of it."

"I'll do my best."

"Have a nice trip, Jake. It may be a long time before I get any liberty." He shakes Jake's hand and goes back to the rail, shouting, "Now liberty call and swim call! All hands going ashore, swim right up to the towline. Liberty call!"

Goodwin goes to the wardroom and opens the dark compartment and shines a light inside. The drenched officers stare at him. They breathe a collective sigh of relief to see it's a lifer of twelve years, Goodwin, coming to save them. He aims his .45 at the bookshelf.

BAM! In the small room the concussion of the big pistol deafeningly stings their ears. The officers are shocked. Some hit the floor. Goodwin gives them a moment to recover and smell the sweet gun smoke and says; "I've got more of those. Anyone want to play grab-ass?"

"Goodwin," says the captain with a firm voice, trying to take charge and open a dialog.

BAM! Goodwin fires a slug into the steel behind the captain's head that ricochets off the wall and blows the coffee urn against a man, hard, but he just grimaces and sweats from the scalding coffee rather than squeal and maybe earn a personal gun-shot.

Now Johanson takes charge of the situation by putting one hand around the captain's neck and pressing his pharynx.

"Okay. What do you want us to do, Goodwin?" says Johanson.

"I don't want to hear no talking, I just want you to file out'a here one by one, five feet apart. Go to the starboard rail, pick up a life jacket, do not put it on, and jump in the water. The gig will pull all of you to shore. Now gentlemen, please move out."

The wet men file out. Johanson says as he files by Jack at the rail, "I'm submitting my letter of resignation in the morning." Jack can't help but smile and say, "I wish *I* could. This is the only way I can resign."

"It's a good ship, sail her well."

"We intend to."

The XO files by and says, "I'm still going to bust you for not marrying that girl."

Jack hands him a packet and says, "Give this demand to the commodore. All we're asking is that this fine ship be kept out of Viet Nam and we want a pardon in exchange for not going to the press with the story of this mutiny. Keep moving."

Tin Can

The captain, following maritime tradition, comes last. Jack breaks his own rule and tries to be a nice guy by explaining to the captain why the world had been turned upside-down.

"You knew the facts of this war and the men didn't. We followed your orders and it was your responsibility to protect us from carrying-out unlawful orders from above. But you didn't even tell us where we were and what we were doing. Led us around blindfolded. Who else could we rely on to protect our honor? That makes you an unlawful commander, unfit for the command of American bluejackets."

Iron-like, they look at each other, wanting to say the right thing to make the other change his mind but they're too far apart.

The captain looks toward the water and gauges his jump. He hates this. A petty officer taking his ship and making him take a dive in front of the crew.

"I relieve you," says Jack. The captain gets a mean sneer on his face which telegraphs his lunge at Jack, who swings his rifle-butt up through the man's legs and drops him to his knees, fixed. Jack takes his collar and drags him like a sack of bad potatoes and rolls him over the side.

"Help that guy out! He can't move! He attacked me, I didn't attack him. There were witnesses. Self-defense."

Holding his mouth above the water, the swimmers move the captain to the swimmers' towline. The gig moves toward shore.

"Well, that's the end of the hostage crisis," says Kaiser.

Jack summarizes, "Yep, the Navy's free to bomb us at will... if they can find us."

"I shit myself," was the first thing Obie said as he drifted back to reality, such as it was. Clean dungarees were no more. Caked black shit in stinky pants. He pulled them off. They stuck to his crotch and ripped pubic hairs out by the roots.

"Damn, you people sure know how to make a guy feel bad," he complimented the unseen captors. He partially stood up. The ceiling was shoulder-height so his head and shoulders stayed bent-over. He took off his blue chambray work shirt and buttoned it around his waste like a kilt. He looked out the little steel-barred window in the door. Across the corridor another eye was looking through its little window. Obie put his fingers in the window and waved "hi." The other eye just looked. Numb or something.

He said to the thing in the opposite cage, "What'cha in here for?"

The other eye said "No talking."

"They put'cha in jail for no talking?"

Unfazed, the eye just looked.

"Have a nice day," said Obie, dismissing the eye.

His box was rough-built plywood. He placed his palms against opposite walls and exerted outward pressure with his back and shoulder muscles. and tested the rest of the wall to find out where the studs were. Twenty-four-inch stud-spacing, not too strong. He knew walls. A summer of construction labor back in high school, just three years ago, was paying-off. "If there's a way to do something, a sailor will find it," he said smiling. "What're they gonna do if I escape? Send me to jail? Hah!"

He sat on the six-inch-high plywood "bed" that covered half the concrete floor of the five-by-five room.

"Is this supposed to scare me, make me ashamed or something? Little plywood doghouse? Hell, I'm ashamed of the Navy. Glad I'm not them."

To get his mind off how badly

patriotic military service was turning out, he remembered a different doghouse, Smokey's. Good old Smokey, a fine Black And Tan fox hound. Clear bugle voice that chimed like a bell when the trail got hot. Nights up on Torch Ridge with the hunters directing their dogs with cow horn trumpets. Bugles and bells ruling the wide-open night. They'd make a campfire while waiting for the chase to develop and gather around the warm light and drink home-made spirits and brag about their dogs, never themselves. The pride and trust you felt in members of the hunt, both dogs and men. He had thought the service would be like that. He laughed at the bitter joke on his younger self. Those guys would not believe what the Navy was doing to him. He imagined them talking about him around the fire:

"Did'ya know they got Obie Oberhoffen locked in some jail in Viet Nam?"

"Nooo." Incredulous.

"Must be a different Obie."

"No, it's ours. They got'im locked-up for takin' drugs."

"If they don't like him, why don't they just send him back?"

"Seem's they wanna treat'im like dog-shit first."

"Let's see what we can do about that. Get'n the truck." And off they'd go. That was what good people did.

Obie saw a mean eye appear in the door view-hole. The lock clicked. The door swung open and a guard rushed in, holding an inflated air mattress in front of him. He fell on Obie and squashed him on the floor and hit him in the mouth, cutting his lips and said, "Tried to get out of the truck today, didn't we? Tried to escape, didn't we? Say you're sorry sir. Say you'll never do it again sir."

Like the people in Bosch's hell-picture, blood flowed from his mouth. He knew the guard wasn't authorized to kill prisoners. He waited for the striking to end. His stomach was hit so hard that it convulsed and retched bitter green bile onto his chest. He went to sleep again.

The eastern Gulf of Tonkin narrows-down to a ten-mile-wide strait between China and Hainan before opening out into the South China Sea.

As dawn breaks, the *Abel* is running at flank speed through the narrows, four miles off the low hills of Hainan and only six miles south of the dark line of the China coast. The weather is good. There are no swells in this shallow and narrow water. The ship charges ahead like a long distance freight train. Thirty nautical miles an hour, every hour. Canton should appear off the bow in ten hours. Ten hours to sanctuary from the threat of death from the power structure from which from which they withdrew their skill and power. The wind whistles in her signal halyards and the blower vents roar.

"Captain" Jack, leader of the mutineers, is on the flying bridge wearing a grim, wind-blown face. Last night was unreal. He wants to verify reality by seeing the sun rise at its appointed time and place and prove that this is not a dream but a day in the life of the world. He looks from one Chinese shore to the other. He opens the cover of the radar repeater and sees the image of the two coastlines but, thankfully, no boats or planes.

Val comes up with an extra cup of coffee. There would be no ships' crews if there were not hot coffee.

"Your strategy's working, Val. No sign of the Navy all night."

"Good. This move is working but they could be waiting on the other side of the straits, out on the China Sea."

"True. After we clear the straits

of Hainan we'll swing north and hug the mainland. They'll know that if they attack us the Chinese will see it on radar and get really nosy. I'll run the ship right up on shore if they damage us. The ship won't sink under the water and the Chinese will salvage it. And us."

"Jack, you know... even if we don't get to Canton, we've won. We won the minute you tossed the captain overboard." They smiled. "We took back our honor in the face of overwhelming odds."

"Yeah, what can they do to us if we've got that. Val... thanks. We couldn't have done it without you."

The sun came out of a pink misty horizon and illuminated a real mutiny.

They were going down the flying bridge ladder when they felt the ship jolt like it ran over a rock. They got to the bridge just as the engine room phone rang.

"The forward engine room's just got a hole in it!" said Starkey.

Jack, flustered, said "What kind of hole?"

"A hole in the bottom! Water's coming in! I think we hit a mine!"

"Well, well, well, hit a mine," said Jack. "How much water's coming in?"

"A lot, like a fire hose."

"How much time we got before it gets to the engine?"

"An hour, tops."

Jack shouts to the helmsman, "Hard right rudder! Steer for the shore! All right. Starkey. Shut down the forward engine room. We're headed for shallow water, we're not gonna sink. How's the after engine room?... Thank god for small favors. Shut down the forward engine and start the pumps and give us time get this sonovabitch aground, okay? Bridge out.

"A mine. A stinking little mine

out here in the middle of nowhere."

Val says, "It was either a stray US mine out of Haiphong Harbor or the US is pulling more secret dirty tricks and starting to mine the approaches to the gulf, too. Once it starts it never ends. We gotta patch it. Somebody's gotta go over the side."

"Well, we've got diving equipment."

"You ever use that kind'a stuff?"

"Don't know a thing about it except you're supposed to use the buddy system when you go diving."

The ship nears the shore and slows to bare steerageway. Mutineers are at the rail peering at the rare sight of bottom ground passing close under an ocean-going ship.

"What's the fathometer say?" Jack asks.

"Still two fathoms."

Jack nervously lights a cigarette. "This is taking too much time. We oughta have someone up front in a boat, taking soundings. Launch the whaleboat and put the gunner in it with a rifle and a sounding line."

The motor whaleboat is launched and moves ahead of the ship, which slowly follows. Goodwin stands in the bow and swings circles with the lead line and lets it fly ahead. He hauls it in as the boat passes over the weight on the bottom. When it's straight up and down he reads the markers and tells his radioman, "Four fathoms."

"This could take forever, we're getting lower in the water all the time," says Jack. "Tell them to head for the beach and visually find twenty-six feet."

The whaleboat makes a full speed run to the beach. Goodwin looks over the side and gauges depth by eye. The boat stops a few hundred yards from the beach, turns around and takes a sounding. It comes back out a few hundred yards and takes another sounding.

"Twenty-six feet, right here," comes the report over the radio. "Sandy bottom."

"All right. Anchor there and wait for us, we're coming in."

The destroyer stops her engines and momentum carries her another hundred yards before she gently runs aground.

Jack says to the men on the bridge, "Anchoring three hundred yards from Chinese soil is going to scare them even more than it scares us. Let's get the hole patched damn quick. Who wants to be Frogman?"

Silence.

"Who's ever gone snorkeling or skin-diving?"

More silence. Jack walks to the bridge wing and shouts down to the boat, "Gunner! You ever been skin-diving?"

"Not me!"

"You ever been swimming?"

"Yes, but I don't know nothing about no skin-diving."

"Come up and get into the gear, we're gonna learn!"

Jack turns to the men and says, "All I know about skin-diving is that it takes two to scuba. Keep a good lookout and keep the guns ready for PT boats out of China." He added, "And planes out of anywhere. We're gonna take a little swim."

The water was cool and bright between the *Abel*'s hull and the sandy bottom. Two divers swam between the propellers and continued under the long gray hull looming six feet above the sand. Amidships, where the generator and pump were located and their noises were the loudest, they found a gash in the ship's hull. They continued their survey and swam past the sonar dome, lodged in the sand at the end of the furrow it had plowed while going aground. They examined the hull to the bow. Jack touched the silent prow as it hovered over the bottom and it looked like the *Abel* was nuzzling the palm of his hand.

They swam back to the boarding ladder and climbed on deck. Jack reported to Starkey, "The hole's like a rip, two feet long and a foot wide. Can you cut a steel plate a foot bigger to put over it?"

"Sure can. I'll be back in ten minutes."

"We'll wait."

A local fishing boat making its daily rounds curved by the *Abel*. The fisherman gawked at the warship stuck in his fishing grounds. Jack waved. The fisherman angled his boat closer and shut off the engine.

"You 'Mellican?" he asked.

"Yes, Mellican."

"You know San Flan Seesko?"

Jack thought. "San Francisco?"

"Yes, yes, I have brodda San Flan Seesko."

"Good, good. Velly good," Jack

said, trying to copy the Chinaman's pronunciation.

"Eet smaw wowald," the man said, making the sign of a little globe with his hands. "You likee feesh?" he said, pointing to some nice snappers in a reed basket.

"Sure! Val, how about getting Pinlicker's brass barometer out of his room and giving it to this nice man for his feesh?"

"Good idea." They made the trade and the fishing boat pulled away and its captain looked back and said, "Good ruck!"

"Ting hai!" answered Jack.

Val sarcastically warned him about being friendly with the natives. "That's one of the "Red Tide" that the National Geographic Magazine warns us about. We're supposed to be very scared."

"Yeah, aren't they the meanest people you ever seen?"

"Ferocious. Very menacing. My

blood runs cold just to think of how...
menacingly evil he was. There he was,
in broad daylight, trying to sell us, get
this, "red" snappers. Oooh."

"Better shoot him before he gets
away."

"Good idea. That's the only
thing that a "menace" can
understand."

Starkey came up and said the
hole was patched and asked, "What're
you guys giggling about?"

"That communist," Jack said,
pointing to the departing fishing boat,
"coerced us into buying *red* snappers."

They chuckled over magazine
propaganda and Jack said, "Let's see if
we can get the old girl out of here."

They engaged the engines in
reverse and kicked-up a lot of sand and
gradually the ship recovered from her
grounding. They backed the *Abel* into
deeper water and resumed course for
Canton.

"Fuck you," groaned Obie, as he floated into consciousness and found the thuggy guard was still beating him.

Obie's curse negated the guard's dominion and broke what little self control he had. In red-burning pure adrenaline frustration he punched Obie too-hard in the chin but his fist glanced off his chin and struck his throat. Obie's larynx broke like an eggshell and he never breathed again.

"Whoops," said the now-fearful guard as he wiped the blood from Obie's lips and tried to give him mouth-to-mouth resuscitation but he couldn't get any air through the crumpled windpipe no matter how hard he blew.

"Oh shit!" he said and fled from the naked corpse in the substandard human kennel.

But Obie's mind wasn't there. It was eight thousand miles away, swooping down from the sky like a Peregrine into the greening branches of the wide Missouri.

The *Abel's* running at flank speed at the end of the Hainan straits. The wide China Sea is ahead. One of the mutineers in Combat has his elbows on a radar screen and his chin on his hands and his eyes are sleepy. He's been on watch for six hours. He blinks at some dots on the screen and rubs his eyes and then clearly sees six blips in a formation that's pointing at the *Abel.* He fumbles for a set of sound-powered phones and puts them on, and blows into the mouthpiece to hear if they're working and reports:

"Bridge, combat."

"Bridge, aye."

"Six unidentified contacts bearing three-five-five, range seven miles."

"Oh God, we'd almost made it. Do you have a speed on them?"

"Yes, I do. Target speed forty-five knots. Looks like torpedo boats."

"Bridge, aye."

"NOW GENERAL QUARTERS, GENERAL QUARTERS FOR SURFACE ACTION!"

The incoming boats aren't visible to the eye but all the big five-inch mounts swing to point at the same spot over the horizon on the port beam, showing something dangerous lies there.

The whining of the steam turbines grows more shrill as thirty knots is forced from the power plant. The bow wave rises and whips across the foredeck like the mane of a horse in wild flight. Men on deck find it impossible to walk against the self-wind and take inside routes to get to their battle stations. Steel hatches and doors clang shut, ventilators shut down. In forty seconds there's no sound but the wailing steam turbines and the train gears of the gun mounts which are keeping their barrels motionless and locked on targets as the ship beneath them surges over the swells at high speed.

Jack's at his station in Combat. "Are you ready, Kaiser?" he says into the phones.

"Kaiser ready."

"Now designating target one," says Jack, putting his hook around the closest boat.

"Locked-on and ready to shoot. Give me the word when you want him erased."

"Kaiser, let's try something. Bring your range in to four miles and lay down a splash line between them and us. See what their intentions are."

BANG! BANG. BANG. A line of exploding water is drawn on the sea in front of the racing boats.

"Targets are turning to avoid shots but have increased speed to fifty knots. They're attacking. They are attacking," announces a radarman.

Kaiser's voice is now nervous over the phones, "You want me to shoot'em?"

"That's a negative, do not shoot yet. I want to try one more thing."

"Bridge, combat," Jack says into the phones. "Hoist the big Chinese ensign to the masthead."

The Chinese flag climbs to the main truck. There is no response from the bouncing boats as their crews try to focus on the *Abel*'s flag signal through wet binoculars.

The radar in Combat shows the boats are spreading apart, going from squadron formation to attack formation, coming in for the kill.

"Kaiser?"

"Kaiser aye."

"Look's like they're coming in. Are you ready for a high rate of fire?"

"Roger that. We're ready."

"It means the end of our Chinese sanctuary plans if we shoot them. Give them one more warning salvo."

BANG, BANG, BLAM!

The boats do not break the attack. Their crews remove the covers from their torpedo tubes in preparation to launch.

"Fantail, Combat."

"Fantail aye."

"Test your noisemaker decoys and stream them now."

On the lurching, wet, rumbling fantail a sailor moves a lever and the electric noisemakers, poised at the edge of the stern, screech like a can of loose ball bearings that's ready to fly apart. He releases the winch brake and the noisemakers pay into the frothy wake.

Three torpedo boats are passing astern of the *Abel* on the outside of their torpedo range. One turns directly onto the ship's wake and bores-in on the ship.

"Kaiser, combat."

"Kaiser, aye."

"Shifting targets. Now designating target two. He's directly astern of us, let me know when you're locked-on."

"Ah-hah, I've got him now. Fire control locked-on target two. I have a firing solution."

"Bridge, Combat. Give the Chinese ensign two big fast dips. We need them more than they need us. I can't believe they'd fire on their own flag."

With a whooshing air blast, one torpedo leaves the torpedo boat and shoots toward the *Abel* and travels under her wake. The fish is doing forty-five knots, overtaking the thirty-six-knot warship at an leisurely nine knots. As the torpedo passes the clattering noisemakers streaming behind the ship, the torpedo's acoustic detonator ignites its warhead.

KaBLoosh! A geyser rises through the foam behind. Everybody on board feels a heavy clank as the shock wave hits the hull.

They have no choice, a shot has

been fired with intent to kill. It's time to respond in kind.

"Kaiser," Jack speaks. "Shoot the bastard."

He sees an indication on radar. "No, no! Wait one moment. Kaiser! Cease fire!"

He looks at the radarman behind the battle plot and raises both hands in a question and points to the plot. The radarman nods vigorous affirmation and draws lines on the plot board showing each of the six attackers is turning away!

"Kaiser, hold your fire! They're breaking it off. Please take your hand off the trigger, they're turning away. They finally saw their own flag at the top of our mast. Bless their little hearts."

The sailors in Combat applaud as the plot board shows the PT boats assuming an escort formation, three on each side of *Abel* and well outside torpedo range.

"Whee-oh! Boys, we got us an honor guard! They thought we were the Navy and were going to kick our ass. Looks like our letter to the authorities got through and China's open. Next stop, Canton! Goodwin, say thank you to the nice PT boats. Fire a star shell high and forward!"

The barrel of mount 51 rises and booms a high shell. White phosphorous on a parachute glows above the rebel destroyer and her six escorts as they exit the straits of Hainan and turn north to the Pearl River and Canton.

When Obie's death is reported to the commander of The Stockade, his face goes slack and he starts raging at the messenger, his top sergeant. "He wasn't here, Blankenship, he wasn't here. We don't *take* Navy guys in here! That's all you know and that's all you say! Burn the place down, burn every stick to the ground. We're gonna start a riot and burn that damn Navy guy's records. Burn his records first! Then make damn sure you burn him and his box to a crisp. Do you hear that? A stinking *crisp!*"

The colonel gets on the phone to headquarters. "We're having a full-scale riot over here, there's going to be a bonfire. Everything's burning right down to the ground. Now listen, very, very carefully. Are you listening? That Navy guy, Oberhoffen, I spell, write this down, are you writing? O-b-e-r-ho- f-f-e-n, was never at this facility. There may be one possible corpse in the ashes that we cannot, I repeat, cannot, and will not, identify in any way, shape or form. So, if you've got one shred of evidence, or if the Navy's got one shred of evidence that that Navy guy was ever here, woe betide the general, woe betide the admirals and the whole fucking war-effort! And most of all, woe betide yourself because I'll get you, so help me God I'll get you to death if you don't do this right. Is that just as clear as the eyes in your mother's head? Good. Now. If you'll excuse me, I've got a riot to conduct."

Half the jail population of two hundred escaped. The other half could have escaped had they enough moxie but instead they stood like zombies in a quiet herd and watched the incineration of their compound as two guards pushed them together. One hundred escapees, hidden by sympathetic Viet Namese, were never re-captured and may be living anywhere in the world. The authorities buried Obie deep in the ashes. His records vanished "through human error" and the world could not learn that Obie died in The Stockade.

Standing on the starboard bridge wing, Jack and Scarputti see the hills of Hainan retreating behind the stern.

"Scarputti, do you think we can trust the Chinese to take us in and give us diplomatic immunity?"

"It's our best risk. We're mutineers, remember? No one has to be nice to us."

"What's it called when a pawn reaches the far end of the board and gets to be anything it wants?"

"Promoted."

"Yeah, promoted. We got to promote ourselves, not just get captured by a different super-power. We need a stunt, something to get the world on our side. Jack gazes at Hainan a moment and says, "How about getting the United Nations in on this? Could we send them a list of rights that sailors should expect as human beings?"

"Sounds good. There should be a bill of rights for military dogs, the most victimized people on earth, next to actual jailbirds, that is."

"Yeah. If we had normal rights, we wouldn't be here, doing this." said Jack, spreading his arms at the stolen ship speeding under them.

"It'd be advantageous to appeal to the U.N. That would give us, and even China, the high moral ground and put the US on the defensive with nothing but medieval laws of serfdom to rely upon."

"Okay, that's our next job, preparing a simple bill of rights to hand to the Chinese and hope they publicize it."

"They might not publish it, Jack. Their record on military rights is probably worse than ours."

"True, very true. Well then, we have to communicate with the world press in Hong Kong to get our message out."

"Yes, we do. That's essential. We can't use the Chinese to talk for us, no one believes their funky censored government news."

Tin Can

"I'm going to write down some rights we needed and later we can figure-out how to get it published."

The door of the XO's cabin slams open and Jack strides in and sweeps the paperwork off the desk. He notices an envelope with "Secret" stamps on it and picks it from the floor and scans it rapidly. It's from an official in the Saigon branch of the Central Instigation Committee:

```
OPERATION PLAN 34-A
   APPROVED ACTIONS
1]Intelligence Collection...
2]Beach    reconnaissance    in
vicinity        of        selected
targets...
3]Physical      Destruction...
SEAL  team  strike  on  dredges
and  buoy  tender  in  Haiphong
Channel...
4]Underwater  Demolition  Team
raid  by  four-man  team    on
SWATOW  torpedo  boats  at  Hon
```

Me. . . .

So, there it is; black and white
proof that your country sent armed
aggressors into another country to
start an international war. Jack is
amazed that such world-affecting and
pivotal acts had been hidden from the
public. They can conceal *any*thing no
matter how big it is. He almost pitied
the president for having to lie to his
citizens about it. He struggled to
believe his country did things like this.
It went against everything he'd been
told about the honest and above board
way that Americans did business. It
hurt inside to know they'd instilled
patriotic pride in him to better use him
as a foolish gladiator for twenty bucks
a week. He chuckled at his former
gullibility. He was relieved of the last
shred of guilt about stealing a Navy
ship. He had conducted the mutiny to
protect his, and other good mens',
consciences and now he finds he did

the right thing on a higher plane, on the plane of international law. His flag and his uniform had been mere colored cloth.

"Here's our defense," he says out loud. "This sheet of paper proves our mutiny was in response to unlawful orders from a rogue authority. It won't save us at a court martial but it'll sure work in a world court and that's where we'll take it... if we survive."

He went to the ship's office and made a hundred photocopies of the damning document. He sat at the yeoman's desk and began typing:

The Enlisted Personnel Bill of Rights
1) Service people shall be advised of illegal orders and freely allowed to refuse illegal duty.
2) An enlistment is not a contract of involuntary

servitude and is terminable at will by either party.
3) High military crimes shall be tried in civil courts in order to protect the rights of Americans in service...

"NOW GENERAL QUARTERS, GENERAL QUARTERS! GENERAL QUARTERS FOR ANTI-AIRCRAFT ACTION!"

A Phantom jet with Navy colors proudly roars past on a flyby, holding its fire. Reflexively, all the gun mounts swing after him, their base rings shrieking in high-speed slew. The smell of burnt kerosene jet exhaust blows across the ship. The escorting PT boats ineffectively spit machine gun bullets at the speeding jets.

Jack arrives at the bridge and Scarputti says, "The flight leader's on the radio, he wants to talk to 'whoever's in charge'."

"Flight leader, this is Knicker Knocker leader," Jack says into the mike. "Come back."

"Knicker Knocker this is Goat Roper. Be advised that the end of the world is near. You are instructed to surrender that US Navy destroyer immediately. I say again, surrender that vessel immediately. Do you copy? Over."

"Listen, you macho bastard, it's *you* that's breathing on borrowed time. The gun director's locked onto your hot ass and has a fire control solution, so just cool your jets and don't make any more threats! Now, do you copy *that*?"

"Roger copy, Knicker Knocker. Uhh, what are your terms for surrender? Over."

"Thank you. We want honorable discharges for all of us and for a shipmate called Oberhoffen who's in the brig somewhere. In return, we'll keep our mouths shut about this mutiny against being forced to commit involuntary manslaughter and illegal US acts of war in the Tonkin Gulf. Over."

"That's a matter for Navy channels to decide but I am instructed to advise you that you'll receive utmost courtesy and clemency if you give up immediately without making us destroy a US government vessel."

"Clemency? At a court martial for mutiny? Gee, that is very believable. Please do not mistake us for idiots. We do not, I repeat, do not, surrender anything."

Scarputti realizes that the Navy's loathe to sink its own ship. "Jack, they don't want to sink us. Call their bluff."

Jack nods.

The flight leader presses his threat. "Knicker Knocker. Listen carefully to my next. I say plainly. Surrender or die, surrender or die. Do you and your men completely understand my instructions? Over."

"Don't give in," says Val. "Tell him the Chinese will get the ship and all our secret stuff."

Jack nods again and says in the radio, "Understand this, Goat Raper or whatever your name is. We're holding *highly* sensitive national security documents called Operation Plan 34A. It appears to be CIA stuff. Ask your superiors what *that* one is all about. We have ten feet of water under the keel and we will not sink below the main deck. We have six escorting Red Chinese PT boats who will rescue personnel *and* salvage secret document 34A and our cryptographic equipment. I respectfully submit that it is *your* ass that is in the sling."

"Knicker Knocker, you are signing a death warrant. This is your last chance to surrender."

"If you do not shut up and get out of here, I'll scuttle the ship myself and make damn sure the Chinese get it!"

He rolls his eyes at Val and goes "Whew" at the stress of lethal gamesmanship.

"Signalman!" Jack shouts back to a man on the signal bridge. "Signal those PT boats to stop firing at the jets."

He says into the sound phones, "Kaiser, do NOT shoot the aircraft. We're playing a bluff and we're afraid that if we make them defend themselves that they'll sink us."

"But they're gonna sink us anyway, they hate us," answers Kaiser in a nervous voice.

"They might and they might not. It's a big career decision for an admiral to sink one of his own warships and give the Chinese secret documents proving that we started the war. Keep tracking the flight leader on air search radar but go passive with your fire control radar. Put the guns straight ahead. We don't want to scare the pilots too much. Kaiser?"

"Yes." "Stay calm, we'll do all right."

"I hope you're right."

"Val, do you think this'll work?" Jack asks.

"There's an apex point in every game where the play has to be bold. If you don't take your main chance, you're not in the game. Whether or not it works, we played it well. That's all we can do. Play well without guarantee of success."

"I'll let the men know what's going on."

"NOW HEAR THIS! We are under the threat of an air attack by the US Navy and we've issued them a counter-threat that we will scuttle the ship and hand it over to the Red Chinese. We think it'll work but if it doesn't and if they attack us, we'll shoot'em down. We're in shallow water within four miles of shore and nobody will drown." He pauses and adds final words, "Whatever happens, the moral victory is ours and always will be. We're free men doing a good job under extreme circumstances. Out."

A pair of jets detach from the high squadron and stoop down to wave-top level. With immense velocity, they bear directly toward the ship. The main guns of the *Abel* are in the home position and don't move, the ship is defenseless. The men are fighting against their instincts to protect themselves and the ship.

The two jets become dots almost touching each other and the ocean as they point directly at the ship and close at a thousand miles an hour. When they're a few hundred yards away they detach two silver canisters which tumble lazily toward the *Abel*'s bow.

SHRIEK-KABOOM! Blasted by concussion, the bridge windows shatter and blow out as the men hit the deck. The ocean turns white, exploding in front of the speeding destroyer. A spray of saltwater rains over the ship as it drives through the blast zone.

"Sheez, those guys are good," says someone from the deck but it's hard to hear him because everyone's hearing is muffled and ringing from the blast.

"What a warning shot. Maybe we'd better give up."

"That's just what they want," says Jack, peeking over the bridge rail at the jets. "Scare us into prison for the rest of our lives with a few bombs. Bombs and prison—the military way of handling personnel problems."

The jet fighters have their afterburners kicked-in and are rising like rockets on tails of thunder.

To strengthen his and the men's resolve, Jack gets on the radio and says, "Hey, Flight Leader. If you happened to notice on your flyby, we have big white 'E's painted on our gun mounts. Those mean that we had perfect scores in gunnery exercises. *We never miss.* That is all."

The men on the bridge smile a little at the bravado and some of their confidence returns.

Suddenly mount 51 jolts into action and slews to track the aircraft. The gun muzzle rises inch-by-inch, exactly tracing the flight of the rising jets.

"Who's doing that!" shouts Jack. "Someone's gonna fire the damn thing off!"

Kaiser's staring at a computer screen that's locked on target and beeping with a fire control solution. A drop of sweat falls from his nose-tip. His hand is on the firing switch and is shaking.

"What'cha doin', Kaiser?" says Jack in Kaiser's phones.

"Those guys are so close together that I can drop'em both with one shot. A two-for-one shot. I never had that before."

Tin Can

Jack breathes deeply and hopes Kaiser hasn't cracked completely under the strain. "I know you can but they could've sunk us with one pop, too. But they didn't. Let'em go, Kaiser. They want us to fire first so they can sink us and claim self-defense. Please, Kaiser, we might wind up as dead meat if you shoot those guys."

The gun muzzle continues following the climbing Phantoms and gradually draws near the bridge wing. Fearful men move away to avoid the impending muzzle blast. Suddenly the gun jerks angrily to the home position and lowers to the deck. The ship's defenseless again.

The two attackers rejoin their squadron, which loiters high, making thirty-mile circles around the mutinous *Abel*.

Except for the rattliing air intake vents to the boilers, it gets quiet. The sky's clear blue and hot. The sea's as calm as an undulating sheet of turquoise satin. The only sound is the running surf from the bow wave and the omnipresent drafting of the stack vents, which the men are used to and don't hear anymore. The world is beautiful in its last few seconds.

"Knicker Knocker!" The tactical radio report bursts onto the bridge.

"Knickers aye," Jack answers quietly.

"You've been granted a presidential pardon subject to the conditions you named. Refuel in Subic Bay, Philippines and proceed to San Diego. Take it home."

The Navy squadron wheels south towards their carrier. The sudden relief from tension breaks Jack's warrior posture. He exhales and plops down on the glass-strewn deck. In a few seconds he recovers enough to simply answer, "Knicker Knocker. Understood."

He reaches up with one hand and pulls the ship's whistle cord and announces on the 1MC with the other hand:

"IT'S OVER, WE'RE FREE! A PARDON HAS BEEN GRANTED."

THOOT-HOOT goes the heavy bass note of the *Abel*'s steam whistle. HOO-OOOO-OOO...

Men throw things around and beat on steel and jump on the shattered glass on the deck and clang the ship's fog bell wildly.

Amidst the cheering, Val reflects on the strategy of his greatest win and says, "I *knew* you would *protect the lie* that you weren't starting a war for pride and profit. You *had* to. I had you *trapped*!"

He makes a fist like he's grasping the man that's been called the most powerful person on earth and bursts into laughter and says, "Our gambit worked so well that now we've got them believing that *we* believe the President will pardon us! Ah ha ha. Sure, we're gonna sail right into the naval base at Olongapo because we *trust* the President. Ooh ha ha ha! I don't believe those guys. HoooWeee! No wonder they're doing so bad in Viet Nam! Play these guys at their own level and they're simple as hell. All they can do is lie and lie some more. No wonder. No wonder at all."

Jack shouts, "We did it! We're freedmen! We beat the Navy! Ya-HOO!" and turns to the helmsman and says, "Head north to the Chinese coast and run about five miles offshore. We're going to Canton!"

Jack shouts over the wing down to Goodwin who's standing beside mount 51, "Finished with guns. Shut'em down!"

Goodwin smiles a smile so big that it squeezes his eyes shut. He gleefully salutes and walks out to the muzzle and puts a tompion in the bore and wrenches it down and throws the wrench high over the bow rail and into the South China Sea. The *Abel* is finished with war.

The Chinese didn't embarrass the U.S. about the Abel mutiny. They were happy enough to document her secrets and exchange her for commercial trade concessions from the U.S. They supplied the mutineers with top-quality identity papers and money and released them. Some slipped back into the States. Some made new homes elsewhere in the world.

Now, whenever I pass by Washington, Columbia, District of, I stop at the National Viet Nam Veterans' Memorial and I walk down that long gray, sad descent into hell, and I touch a certain name in The Wall and it's like touching him again:

GERALD WAYNE OBERHOFFEN

"We'd never have done it if it weren't for you, old buddy, old lone shipmate who dared to deny your services to the government when the government was wrong."

Delores and I are married now and she understands why I carry a handkerchief and she steps away and I stand there wishing – that Obie had been able to come home with us.

finis

Printed in Great Britain
by Amazon

16399969R00133